Make a Wish

SANDRA BYRD

BETHANYHOUSE

MINNEAPOLIS, MINNESOTA

Make a Wish
Copyright © 2001
Sandra Byrd

Cover illustration by Bill Graf
Cover design by Lookout Design Group, Inc.

Published by Bethany House Publishers
A Ministry of Bethany Fellowship International
11400 Hampshire Avenue South
Bloomington, Minnesota 55438
www.bethanyhouse.com

Printed in the United States of America by
Bethany Press International, Bloomington, Minnesota 55438

Library of Congress Cataloging-in-Publication Data

CIP data applied for

ISBN 0-7642-2481-6

Praise for *Cross My Heart,*
THE HIDDEN DIARY, book 1

Cross My Heart was *very* descriptive (but not, like, overloaded!) and fun. It's a touching story that a lot of girls can relate to because of their own busy parents. I liked the mystery, too!

> Lilly, eleven years old, daughter of Liz Curtis Higgs,
> author of *Bad Girls of the Bible*

Mama mia! *Cross My Heart* was a great book! I liked the way the author left you hanging at the end of each chapter. It made you want to keep reading. I could really relate to some of the characters, and Claudette made me laugh. You'll love this book! Cross my heart!

> Tavia, ten years old, daughter of Deborah Raney,
> author of *A Vow to Cherish* and *Beneath a Southern Sky*

This book was really good, interesting, and fun. I couldn't say I had one favorite part because I loved the whole book! I couldn't put it down.

> Tyler, eleven years old, daughter of Lisa E. Samson,
> author of *The Church Ladies*

I couldn't put this book down! I guarantee you'll love *Cross My Heart,* and it will keep you on the edge of your seat.

> Marie, thirteen years old, daughter of Terri Blackstock, author of the NEWPOINTE 911 series

Cross My Heart is a very exciting book. Lucy . . . meets new friends and learns about God. I know my friends will love this book like I did. Maybe we'll find a hidden diary somewhere, too.

> Madelyn, nine years old, daughter of Cindy McCormick Martinusen, author of *Winter Passing*

I think Lucy and Serena are really cool. I can't wait to read the next HIDDEN DIARY book.

> Bethany McHenry, nine years old,
> daughter of Janet Holm McHenry,
> author of *PrayerWalk* and *Girlfriend Gatherings*

Books by
Sandra Byrd
FROM BETHANY HOUSE PUBLISHERS

Girl Talk

THE HIDDEN DIARY
Cross My Heart
Make a Wish
Just Between Friends
Take a Bow

To Debbie Austin:
Make new friends but keep the old.
One is silver and the other gold.

Contents

Opening the Diary

Saturday morning . . . D Day minus six

High above the sidewalk the girls walked upon, the palm trees tossed their leafy heads back and forth in the salty sea breeze. Lucy glanced at Serena out of the corner of her eye; Serena looked back and smiled. They giggled together and started walking even faster. In less than two minutes they'd be sprawled on the beach, under the yellow umbrella, ready to begin their secret summer adventures.

"You did bring the diary. . . ." Lucy said.

"It's right here!" Serena tapped her straw beach bag.

Inside that bag, Lucy knew, was the old diary she and Serena had found last week. More than seventy years ago, Serena's great-grandma, also named Serena, had written in that diary with her best friend, Mary. The key and clues had been in the home Lucy's family was renting this summer; the diary had been in Serena's house.

The girls' four hands smoothed the blanket across the sand. Serena opened up the umbrella, casting a shadow across half the blanket. As Lucy reached to turn on some music, another shadow appeared.

"Hi."

Lucy looked up and saw a tall girl towering above them, her long brown ponytail still swishing even though her feet were firmly planted.

"Hi, Julie," Serena said, her voice disappearing into the breeze.

Lucy's arms freckled with goose bumps. She never took her eyes off of Julie.

"I didn't know you were coming to the beach today. Why didn't you call to invite me?" Julie looked at Serena, ignoring Lucy. Lucy tucked her strawberry blond hair behind her ear and fiddled with the radio. She wasn't going to fake a smile at Julie and beg her to be friends, that was for sure. A hot flush covered her face even though she hadn't been in the sun long.

"Oh. Well, we just normally show up and see who's here, right? And you're here anyway," Serena answered.

Julie wedged herself between Lucy and Serena, turning her back to Lucy. Lucy casually drew the bag with the diary in it as far away from Julie as she could. She and Serena had decided to read the contents only with each other—as Serena's great-grandmother had wanted.

"I'm waiting for Jenny to come back on the ferry," Julie said. "She went over town yesterday to celebrate her birthday at her aunt's house. She just turned twelve." Julie looked at Lucy.

Maybe she's going to be nice to me after all.

"I'm going to be twelve this coming week, too," Lucy offered.

"Who cares?" Julie turned her back again.

Lucy pinched her lips together to corral some harsh words. She squeezed her eyes together, too, to keep back something else.

"Anyway, I'm sitting over there with Erica and Amy, in case *you*"—she nodded to Serena—"want to join us." She pointed to a group of girls staring at them.

"Thanks, maybe later," Serena said. Julie stood up and walked away, her heels spitting a trail of sand behind her.

Lucy opened her eyes, emotions controlled now. "Mama mia, they need better pest control at this beach," she muttered. She cleared her throat to get rid of the unwelcome warble.

"Don't worry," Serena said. She looked toward the nearby crowd.

Lucy followed her gaze. "Am I keeping you from your other friends? I mean, I'm new here, and you've been friends with them a long time."

"No! I can hang out with them, too. And so can you. Don't worry."

Lucy raised her eyebrows but said nothing.

"And today," Serena said, "is *our* day. Our day to finally open and read the diary and plan some fun!"

Lucy slid her sunglasses on and smiled. "Yeah. Adventures await." She rolled onto her stomach to warm her back and doodled in the sand.

Serena scooted next to her. "Let's wait till they move a

bit farther away before opening the diary, okay?" she whispered.

Lucy nodded.

Serena drew a face in the sand.

"You're really good!" Lucy admired the picture, a cat.

"Thanks," Serena said. "Drawing in the sand reminds me of the alphabet beach game. Want to play?"

"Of course—I'm always up for fun," Lucy said. "Bring it on!"

"Well," Serena propped herself on an elbow. "We have to pick a category: Eager or Afraid."

"Afraid sounds more daring," Lucy said. She propped herself up, too.

"We start with A. I have to write something starting with the letter A that I'm afraid of." Serena bit her lip and twirled her long, almost-black hair. Lucy sighed. Oh, to have smooth, glossy hair like that. Serena was so pretty, but she didn't seem to know it.

Serena wrote out *Art Fair*. Then she looked up at Lucy.

"What does that mean?" Lucy asked gently.

"In a couple of weeks there's going to be an art show on the Island called Art Fair," Serena explained. Catalina Island, where the girls were spending the summer, was about twenty-five miles off the coast of Los Angeles. Serena's family had spent every summer here for many generations. Lucy's family was visiting this summer only, while her dad researched plant life for his job.

"Cool!" Lucy said.

"Well, my brother, Roberto, and his band are going to

perform. He told my mom he thought I should show some of my drawings," Serena said.

"Great! So what's the problem?"

"The last time I tried to show some pictures at my old school fair, they turned me down. My art wasn't good enough." Serena cast her eyes down. "I'm afraid that if I show everybody my drawings now, they'll laugh at me. I never show them to anyone anymore."

"But—" Lucy started to say something, when Serena jumped in.

"Your turn! You have to write something *you're* afraid of that starts with the letter B."

Lucy twisted the rings on her fingers. *B.* She looked at the girls sitting over by Julie, who were picking up their things as the ferry began to pull into the harbor.

"Jenny's back!" someone called out.

Lucy traced the letters B-E-L-O-N-G on the sand.

"What do you mean?" Serena looked puzzled.

"I don't ever really belong," Lucy said softly, tracing and retracing over the letters. "My mom and dad separated last year, and I didn't feel right with either of them without the other. They're back together now, working on things. But I'm afraid that might happen again. I'm an only child, so I'm with adults a lot. Which feels weird. And now I'm here for the summer. Another place I don't belong."

"But—" Serena started to say. This time Lucy changed the subject.

"Come on, they're gone now. Let's open the diary! We've been waiting for this for *days!*" She snagged the woven beach bag from the far corner of the blanket.

The girls sat up and put their heads close as the wind blew their hair together. Lucy scooted close to Serena. "You open it. It was in your family, after all."

"But you found the letter and the key!" Serena protested. "Without them, there would be no diary discovery!"

"Nope," Lucy handed it over. "But I'll sit really close so we can read it together."

Serena opened the thin red diary to the first page and read, *"The Diary of Serena and Mary, Faithful Friends, Summertime, 1932."*

The spine creaked open and the pages flapped.

"Let's only read till *almost* the end," Lucy said. "That way we can see what happens in our adventure this week without knowing the ending to theirs. It'll be a surprise!"

When they found the diary a few days before, the girls had agreed to read one section each week, just like the diary had been written. Then—no matter what trouble or fun or excitement or worries—Lucy and Serena would try to do something just like the girls in the old diary did all those years ago. They'd have only six days each week till D Day, the day that week's Diary Deed must be done before they were on to a new adventure.

"Okay." Serena began to read out loud.

"Week One.
Dearest Diary,
    We Faithful Friends are here to tell you good news—a party! We're having it at The Swordfish Club, because there's not enough room in my house or Mary's to have all of our friends over. We girls

are going to dance the one-step even, because mary's cousin has a radio and can teach us. We're going to listen to music from 'High atop the Plaza Hotel in New York City!' ”

Serena stopped reading. "You read the part where the handwriting changes."

Lucy nodded and eagerly picked up where the handwriting changed. "That must mean Mary's writing now!

"Serena is sooo happy, because she loves parties, though I might rather stay home and read. But that wouldn't do. A party it is, and Serena says it will be a panic! I hope the radio works. Sometimes it doesn't. It would be simply awful to invite everyone over to learn a dance and then have the radio ball up. But we've already promised, so we must have music!"

"It sounds like their summer was starting out really, really fun." Lucy laughed. "If their radio doesn't die, that is."

The girls read the next page, all about the plans of who would be coming and what the theme would be and how they hoped it would all pull off swell, although they disagreed over whether they should have a back-up plan for the radio. Just at the part where they came back to describe if they pulled off a successful party after all, Serena closed the diary.

"It's settled, then," she said.

"What's settled?" Lucy asked.

"We'll have a party."

Lucy's eyes opened wide. "A party?"

Serena smiled. "We did say that we were going to do whatever they did, right?"

Lucy sighed. "Couldn't we just listen to some big band music or something?" *A party means inviting . . . others.*

Serena began putting things away in the bag. "Nope. Where's your courage, Miss Bravery? And I think it should be a birthday party. With other girls. For you."

"For me? With other girls? Uh-uh. Nope. Who would even come?" Lucy glanced over at the place where Julie and the others had been, the impressions from their bodies still fresh in the sand.

"Oh, lots of them. I'll give you the names," Serena said. "Come on, we've got a lot of work to do, Lucy! It's perfect! Isn't your birthday on Friday?"

Lucy nodded.

"Friday it is! Friday's D Day. It couldn't get more exciting." Serena folded the umbrella. "We don't even have to dance the one-step."

Lucy looked at her friend's eager face.

"I don't even *know* the one-step!" Lucy said, tucking the diary into the beach bag.

A real birthday party. My first.

Her heart thumping, Lucy ran her hand across the letters B-E-L-O-N-G she'd drawn in the sand, now erasing them forever.

Fiesta

Saturday afternoon . . .

"Hey, Mom!" Lucy kicked off her flower-power sandals, warm feet pressing against the cool floor tile as she and Serena stepped into the summer cottage.

"I'm in here," Lucy's mom called from the living room. It wasn't really a living room anymore. Mom's easels, lamps, and supplies had fought for and conquered most of the room. A green velvet sofa and a couple of lumpy chairs cowered against the walls.

Lucy plopped down in a chair and wrinkled her nose. *Linseed oil. Mom must be painting with oils today.*

"Hello, Mrs. Larson," Serena said politely, eyes never leaving the canvas on the easel. She nearly knocked a floor lamp onto Lucy's head as she tried to get to a chair to sit down. "Oh, I'm so sorry," she said.

"Never mind. I'm sorry about the room," Lucy said quietly.

Serena's eyes opened wide. "Don't apologize! This is

great. You didn't tell me your mother was an artist."

"Yeah, well," Lucy said.

"What have you girls been up to today?" Lucy's mother asked, not looking up.

"Mom!" Lucy said. "We read the diary, of course! Did you forget?"

Her mother put down her brush and wiped a wisp of hair from her face with the back of her hand, smearing a bit of blue across her cheek. She smiled. "I did forget. But now I'll sit down and hear all about it." She sat on a chair next to the girls.

"Well, it was great, just as we hoped it would be. They talk funny but kind of cool, and they like to listen to music, like we do."

Mom rolled her eyes. She and Lucy did not like the same kind of music. "What else?"

Lucy's voice thinned. "Well, they had a big party, I guess."

"And we'd like to have one, too!" Serena jumped in. "For Lucy's birthday! A big Catalina birthday bash! Isn't that fun?"

"Oh." Lucy's mother pursed her lips. "Well, it might be. We've always just gone out to dinner for Lucy's birthday, being that we're always away in the summer."

"That's why I thought this would be so fun. *Fiesta!*" Serena's Spanish slipped out. "If that's all right with you, I mean."

"Is that what you want, Lucy?" her mom said.

"At first I wasn't sure," Lucy spoke up. "But, well, it might be kind of fun to have a couple of kids there, too."

"A *lot* of kids!" Serena said. "It'll be big!"

Does a lot of kids mean everyone? Do I have to invite everyone?

"I've never done a kid's birthday party before. I never knew what to do with a lot of kids. I could try, though." Mrs. Larson warmed up to the idea. "It might be kind of nice. I could order some sandwiches or something."

Serena's eyebrows drew together like chopsticks. "Well, maybe we could think some more about the food, you know? And a theme!"

"How about, 'Stranded on a Majorly Dangerous Island With Crazy Flesh-Eating Natives,' for a theme," Lucy said, only half joking.

"That's it! An island party. Terrific," Serena said, not getting the point. "And," she said to Mrs. Larson, "I'll help with the food ideas, too. But we'd better get going. The party is in six days!"

"Mmm-hmm," Lucy's mother said. "We can't have it here, though."

"What?" Lucy and Serena said together.

"There's no room for a group." She swept her hand through the air of the small space.

Lucy nodded and looked at her feet.

Her mom put her hand on Lucy's shoulder. "Why don't you go to Dad's office and see if he has any ideas. He's more of a party person than I am, anyway."

"All right," Lucy said. She ran the old diary up to her room and grabbed her Jelly Belly case. Then she ran back downstairs. "Let's go!"

Out the door and down the street, Lucy opened her

Jelly Belly case. "No lunch yet. I'm hungry. Want a peanut-butter-and-jelly sandwich?"

"You have one?"

Lucy grinned and handed Serena one each of Grape Jelly and Peanut Butter Jelly Bellies. "This will hold you over." She popped two into her own mouth, too, squashing them between her teeth. Then she slipped the thin case back into her pants pocket.

When they got to her dad's office a few blocks later, Serena stared.

"*This* is your dad's office? Wow!" Two big cacti and a fireweed bush flanked the doorway of the large building.

"It's not too bad," Lucy admitted. "It used to be a rich person's house, and the university bought it." She pushed the door open and walked into the front room.

"Hi, Lucy!" Seven-year-old Claudette jumped off of her dad's computer chair and ran to hug Lucy. "Hi, Serena!" Claudette hugged Serena, too, who raised her eyes at Lucy. Lucy winked and tousled Claudette's hair.

"Whatcha doing, Claudette?" she asked.

"Playing computer games. And I just wrote a letter to my grandma. I used spell check. Cool, huh?" Claudette waved the letter at Lucy.

"Cool, Claudette." Lucy looked around the office. "Is your dad here? Is my dad?"

"They're out back."

Claudette's dad worked with Lucy's dad doing plant research each summer for the university where they both taught. Claudette jumped back into the chair, looking like Goldilocks swallowed in Papa Bear's chair. Her bright orange socks had nothing in common with her red dress. Lucy giggled. Claudette and her socks.

Then Claudette turned back to her computer game.

Lucy motioned to Serena, and they walked out onto the back patio.

The patio was wide, with a brown thatched roof over a whitewashed ceiling. It looked like it came from the South Pacific movies Lucy's Grammy loved to watch. There were wicker rockers and thick flowering vines curled around the columns and corners. Ripe flowers littered the patio floor, spilling their perfume into the air. The patio opened onto a wide, grassy plain that sloped onto the beach.

"Hi, Dad!" His beard bristled against Lucy's lightly freckled skin as she kissed his cheek.

"What's up, Sparky?"

"Serena wants to have a birthday party for me on Friday night. The girls in the diary had a party, so we have to have one, too. Mom said maybe you'd have an idea where to have one."

"A party!" Dad's eyes gleamed. "Of course. A party!"

"With an island theme," Serena said.

"Can I dance?" her dad teased.

"Dad!" Lucy said before she saw he was teasing. "Only if I can videotape it for blackmail purposes," she teased back.

"Well then, how about right here?" he suggested. "I could set up a little barbecue, a whole pig would be nice. And then I could arrange some umbrellas and—"

"Dad." Lucy held her hand up. The one bad thing about Dad was he always tried to take over everything. "I think it would be great to have it here." She looked at Serena, who nodded. "But *we* can plan it ourselves. Really."

"Oh, all right," he replied. "I can help with whatever you need."

Claudette must have overheard; she raced in from the other room. "Can I come? Please? I love parties!"

Lucy looked at her dad. Claudette's dad saw the look and spoke up right away.

"I think it will probably be past your bedtime, honey," he said. "We'll see Lucy earlier in the day on her birthday. Okay?"

Claudette's shoulders sank.

"And I'll take you pedal boating on Monday afternoon. How's that?" Lucy added.

Claudette nodded.

Lucy spied a box of bottles in the corner. "What are those?"

"Bottles we used for seawater samples," her dad answered. "Why?"

Lucy stepped over to the box and took one out. She tipped it on its side and looked at Serena through it. "I'm glad you didn't throw these out. They're perfect for invitations!"

"Hey . . ." Serena said, the light turning on in her eyes. "Those would be awesome for messages in a bottle. A message in a bottle is a *great* way to send an important note. It practically says, 'Pay attention to this!' And with an island theme . . ."

"Exactly. With some sand—and a note asking them to come—these will be perfect invitations," Lucy said, growing excited. Her first birthday party! She had never, ever had a birthday party before, not in eleven years. Her mom said she didn't know what to do with a lot of kids, and then, well, they were always away. Lucy's heart floated to think she might really have a party after all. With . . . friends.

"You can have the bottles," her dad said. "I've got cases of them in the storage room in the back. How many do you need for invitations?"

Lucy looked beyond the patio, beyond the smooth green grass doing the hula in the summer breeze. Her gaze stopped at the wide-brimmed, sandy beach. A group of girls walked back from the ferry landing, along the foamy water. One girl, in the center, tossed her long brown ponytail and made sure everyone trailed after her.

Lucy thought she knew who it was.

"Well, you'll need about ten—one for me to keep and one for you to keep and then enough to invite everyone I've introduced you to," Serena said. "Are you going to invite everyone?"

Lucy didn't answer right away, never taking her eyes off of the beach crowd.

Sleepover

Sunday night . . . D Day minus five

"Do you think we should go downstairs and ask your mom if we can start?" Serena asked the next evening, blowing at the wet paint on Lucy's fingernails. Serena's overnight gear was tossed on the twin bed to the left, just across from Lucy's bed. In her sloped, attic closet was the built-in dresser where the letter and diary key had been hidden all these years.

Two droopy plants sagged on the corner of the dresser, and a load of dirty clothes peeked out from under Lucy's bed.

Lucy frowned. "I haven't seen much of my mom all day. They had a Bible study this morning, and then she's been painting all afternoon with the door shut." Lucy's chest tightened. Her mom used to paint behind closed doors all the time—*before*. But Mom had *promised* to make this more of a family summer.

"She told me to wait for her before making the party

invitations, though." Lucy checked her watch. "Let's give her half an hour and then we'll go down there."

"Are you nervous about the invitations?" Serena asked.

Lucy nodded but said nothing.

"Come on, I have something fun to show you." Serena grabbed Lucy's hand and pulled her into the bathroom, closing the door behind them. "Now turn off the light."

"What are you doing?" Lucy turned the light off, and Serena closed the blinds against the stars and the moon.

"Okay, kneel down by the toilet and watch while I flush," Serena told her.

"Have you lost your mind?" Lucy asked, giggling, but she did as she was told.

Serena flushed the toilet, and as Lucy watched, hundreds of tiny little dots of light lit up the water in the bowl.

"Wow!" Lucy stared as they swirled away. "Awesome. What is that?"

"The water for plumbing is right from the ocean. There are little electric water bugs that are so tiny you can't see them in the water. But they glow in the dark when they're moved. Roberto showed me."

"The drinking water, too?" Lucy asked, grossed out.

"Nope. But if you draw in the sand at night, it lights up, too," Serena said.

"Let's try it one night!" Lucy said.

They walked back to Lucy's room and played one of Serena's Christian CDs. Lucy's throat ached as Serena closed her eyes and sang. *What would it be like to feel that close to God?*

"I went to church today. Did you?" Serena asked.

Lucy shook her head. "My parents want us to go next week."

"Do you want to go?" Serena asked.

"I think so. I feel funny. I haven't been in a church for a long time."

Just then Lucy's mother knocked on the door.

"Come on down!" Lucy and Serena trailed her into her painting room. Spread across the coffee table were fifteen hand-painted watercolors. Each one was on a thin slip of paper, with a light blue sea wash and hibiscus flowers all around. In the center was painted: *Please Come. A Birthday Party for Lucy Larson. Friday Evening, 7:00 P.M.* Then she'd painted the address of the office. One of the watercolors was rolled into a little scroll so the girls could see how the invitations would be slipped into the bottles; she'd left the others open so they could see her work.

Serena stared at the open invitations while Lucy fell back into the couch with the broken springs.

"Mom! Is this what you've been doing all day?"

Her mother's smile faded. "You do like them, don't you?"

Lucy jumped up and squeezed her mother. "I *love* them."

"Well, I'm not very good with kids, but I can paint," Mom said, grinning again.

"I'll say you can paint. I wish I could paint like this."

"Do you paint?" Mrs. Larson turned toward Serena with interest.

Serena nodded. "But I *never* show anyone. I draw and paint on scraps and throw them away."

Lucy's mom stepped over to her desk and picked up a sketchbook. "Don't throw them away. Sketch them in a book like this, or an ordinary notebook, and save them. You don't have to show anyone, but I bet if you do, you'll be surprised." She set the leather sketchbook down. "And you'll see your own growth as an artist."

Serena looked at it longingly, then turned toward Lucy. "Well, we'd better get moving. We have to stick the scrolls into the bottles and then put them into the little boxes and put addresses on them. No time to waste. They've got to be delivered tomorrow if anyone is going to RSVP!"

"Oh." Lucy's mother sat down. "I never throw parties, and I forgot about painting an RSVP." She looked at the invitation. "I don't think there's room."

"Don't worry, Mom," Lucy rushed in. "I'm *so* glad you did these for me. They're perfect. In fact," she thought for a second, "I wouldn't even want an RSVP. There's hardly any time between then and now. Whoever shows up just does. Like the open house at school last year. I'll just tell them that when I deliver them tomorrow."

Mom smiled again.

Tomorrow. Lucy looked at the clock, a big white eyeball with numbers staring down from the wall. Less than twelve hours away. Lucy had wanted a real summer with other kids. She just didn't know it was going to be so hard.

The two girls raced up the stairs, each cradling an armful of scrolls. They set them down on Lucy's wooden bedroom floor, between Lucy's bed and the guest bed. Then they started stuffing them into the bottles.

"I guess we don't really need addresses, since I know

where everyone lives," Serena said.

Lucy set down her scroll. "I've been meaning to talk with you about that."

Serena stopped, too. "What?"

"Well," Lucy started, "I think I should go and deliver them myself. Not that I wouldn't *love* to have you there, believe me. But since it's my *birthday* party, I kind of want people to come because they *want* to. Not just because they don't want to hurt *your* feelings. I . . . I can't be friends with them on my own if I don't try first."

Serena looked at her. "I see. Okay."

"You're not mad, are you? It will still be our party. I wouldn't have even had one without you. We can do all the other stuff together."

"I'm not mad," Serena said. "It's definitely *your* birthday party. And I understand how you feel; I'd probably feel the same way. We'll do all the food and music and decorating together. You can use my name if you want to when you're talking with them."

Lucy squeezed her friend's hand. "Thanks. I hope I won't need to."

Serena stood up and set some of the bottles on Lucy's dresser. "Sorry about the plant." She lifted one limp leaf of a potted violet.

"Everything I try to grow I kill in record time."

"But your dad's a plant scientist!" Serena giggled.

"That just makes it worse, believe me," Lucy said.

"How cute!" Serena picked up a photo next to the plant. "Cool frame."

"Thanks," Lucy said. "Another thrift-shop find. You

can't believe what some people throw away."

"Who's the dog?" Serena pointed to the picture inside the frame.

Lucy lowered her eyelashes. "That was my pooch, Jupiter. He died last year. He wasn't very old."

Serena knelt down. "I'm sorry."

"I'm going to save all of my birthday money to buy a new dog when we get home," Lucy said. Her face brightened. "I want a pet named after every planet in the solar system before I go to college."

Serena giggled and yawned. "Who's next? Astro Dog?"

"That's not a planet, goofy!" Lucy slipped the last bottle into its box and began writing her return address on the boxes. "So people know where I live, in case they want to ask me something," she said.

"I'll write the addresses on the boxes for you, so you know where to deliver them," Serena said. Her handwriting was artsy and beautiful. She wrote out almost all of the addresses, reading from a handwritten note she'd brought from home with all of the girls' names, numbers, and addresses.

Finally Serena held up the last box. "Last one. For Julie. Going to invite her?"

Lucy looked at the box. She looked at her hands and twisted her rings. She looked at the glow-in-the-dark cross Claudette had stuck to her mirror last week. She looked at the floor. "Yes," she finally answered. "I'll invite her. I know what it feels like to be left out."

Serena addressed the last box, then the two of them put

on their PJs, said good-night to Lucy's parents, and crawled into their beds.

"Can I pray out loud?" Serena asked.

"Sure," Lucy answered. Serena prayed for both of them, then yawned again and turned over in bed.

Lucy punched and squashed her pillow into a ball before resting her head on it.

"I hope someday I feel as close to Jesus as you do."

"You can!" Serena said. "Just reach out and do it."

I don't know how to reach out and do it.

Lucy prayed in her heart and felt peaceful for a bit. Then she let the thoughts about the party—and whether anyone would show—take over again.

She tried to sleep, but she kept noodling her legs and arms and covers, never finding just the right spot. The moonlight and the scent of the sea both slid in through the window screen. Lucy stared at the boxes of invitation bottles, standing at attention in a row on her dresser.

"Tomorrow's the day, isn't it?" Lucy whispered across the room. "I'll find out what everyone says."

Serena's even, quiet breathing was the only answer.

Special Delivery

"I thought you were going to deliver the invitations first thing this morning." Lucy's dad swept some toast crumbs from the table into his hand and dumped them into the sink. He opened the wooden blinds to welcome the morning sun.

"Mom says not to visit people we don't know before ten o'clock," Lucy replied. "And Serena just left." Lucy popped the last piece of hard-boiled egg into her mouth with a flourish. It jiggled between her teeth for a minute, and then she swallowed. "Besides, I've got a great idea! I just decided like, forty seconds ago."

Her dad grabbed his case. "What's that?"

"I'm going to *mail* them! They're already in boxes; I just need to add stamps. It will be so much more exciting for people to get some mail. Don't you think?"

Her dad smiled and leaned over for a kiss good-bye. "And that way you won't have to deal with possible rejection face-to-face, huh?"

Lucy's face tightened. "Well, there is that, too."

"I'll pray for you," he said as he walked out the door.

"Thanks, Dad . . ." her voice trailed after him.

Lucy crammed the dishes sideways into the crowded dishwasher and slammed the door before her mom came down and saw how full it was. She turned the knob on and headed toward her room.

After running her hands through her hair, she noticed in the mirror the flash of pearl pink Serena had painted on her nails last night. It looked . . . cute.

Straining to carry the beach bag with the invitations, Lucy practically dragged them down the stairs.

"I'm going, Mom," she said.

"Okay. See you in a bit," her mother called from her room. "Don't forget your radio!"

Lucy checked to see that her two-way radio was clipped onto her shorts and that she had her money, then she headed out the door to the post office.

This is *a good idea*, she decided. *Mail is very fun to get. It'll be great.*

She walked the two blocks to the Avalon post office, watching the tourists arrive for the day from the ferry dock. Floppy hats, swinging cameras, and khaki shorts were dead giveaways.

Lucy smiled to herself. *I'm thinking of* them *as tourists, but myself as an Islander. Maybe I* am *getting to be an Islander, and I've only been here a week and a half!*

Through the narrow alley and into the post office Lucy hauled the heavy sack. After waiting in line long enough for what seemed like two birthdays, she finally heaved it onto the counter.

"I'd like these to go first class," she said to the clerk.

The lady's head was down, but her eyes peeked over her half-moon glasses as she read the addresses.

"These are all Avalon addresses," she said.

"Yes." Lucy looked confident.

"We don't deliver to Avalon street addresses," the lady said. "Only post office boxes. Everyone has to pick up their mail at a P.O. Box." She shoved the invitations back toward Lucy. They nearly fell off the counter.

"Oh. I didn't realize that." Lucy thought she heard people in line begin to clear their throats and shuffle their feet a bit, making noise. *I thought my family had a P.O. Box because we're visitors.*

The clerk looked at the growing line behind Lucy. "Would you like to go home and get all of the P.O. Box numbers and bring them back?"

"I don't know," Lucy said. The woman behind her coughed loudly. A baby started to wail.

"Sometimes Islanders don't pick up their mail but once a week. If it's something important, you might want to know that."

Lucy wrapped the bag handles around her wrist and lifted the sack down. "Thank you anyway."

The woman behind her had her mail on the counter before Lucy had even left. "Two Priority Mail," she barked as Lucy pushed the door open from the post office. Winding through the narrow alley once more, she soon arrived at an outside bench.

Now she felt dumb. Lucy hadn't seen a mailman since she'd been on Catalina. A piece of gum caught on the bottom of her shoe as she sat down. Once sitting, she slid to the middle of the bench so she wasn't sitting on the dried, dripped ice cream on one half or the bird doo on the other.

Lucy set the bag down in front of her and reached one hand around to pull her hair off of her sweaty neck. As she did, her thumb caught on the thread of her beaded necklace. It snapped, and the tiny colored beads rolled like rainbow tears in every direction—under the bushes, into the street, in the sidewalk crack, down the water drains.

What more could go wrong? She sighed and tossed the necklace string down the water drain, too. *Some Islander I am if I don't even know they don't deliver mail. Might as well go home and get back to plan A. Or B . . . or Z.*

After plodding home and setting the bag inside the door, she kicked off her flower-powers and went into the kitchen.

"Want an early lunch?" her mom asked, chopping something next to the sink. Egg-salad smells stink-bombed the room.

"Not really hungry," Lucy said.

"How'd it go?"

"It didn't. They don't deliver mail to street addresses."

"Ah," her mother said. "I thought you were going to deliver them in person." She tugged and jiggled and tried to jerk open the dishwasher. "*Why* is this dishwasher always stuck? Argh!"

Lucy held her breath for a minute, and then her mother

yanked it open, grabbed a spoon, and turned back to lunch-making.

"I *was* going to deliver them. Then I changed my mind." Lucy wandered over to the refrigerator and took out a Dr Pepper.

"You had a good sleepover last night, though, right?"

"Great!" Lucy perked up. "We had a lot of fun. Maybe I should just scrap this birthday party and do something fun with Serena."

"That's okay with me," her mom said. "You know how I am." She stirred some mayonnaise into the chopped eggs. "But easier isn't usually your way. And what about copying the old diary?"

Lucy poured the Dr Pepper over ice, watching the fizz rise to the top, the cherry-chalky smell tickling her nose.

"Speaking of sleepovers," Mom said, "do you remember when you went to the cousins' sleepover with Katie last year?"

"Of course!" Lucy giggled. "All of her cousins from her other side of the family were there—and then there was *me*! The stranger!"

"And of course we got there late."

"And of course there wasn't any room left on the family room floor."

"So you . . ." her mom started.

"I wiggled between some of the others! I said 'excuse me' and set my sleeping bag down and shared my Jelly Bellies and started to talk."

"And what did they do?"

"Once I made a place for myself, they made a place for me. We had fun."

Lucy's mother raised her eyebrows.

Lucy nodded. "I see. Thanks, Mom." Then she smiled. "I guess I'll grab the map and go deliver the invitations in person. Save some egg salad for me!"

"You'd better get moving if you want anyone to come. It's four days away!" Lucy raced out the door, packing the bag of invitations on her back like Santa Claus's loot.

"And don't forget you promised to take Claudette pedal boating today!" her mother called after her.

Green Skin

Early Monday afternoon . . .

Once out the door, Lucy didn't feel as brave as she had a few minutes before. "Might as well start with the easy one." Lucy hiked the two blocks to Betsy's house. Betsy at least knew her a little; she'd had a great time last week pedal boating with Betsy. And Betsy's little sister seemed to have taken to Claudette like a barnacle to a boat.

Lucy knocked twice.

"Hi, Lucy! Do you want to come in?" Betsy opened the door, her long braids hanging down her back like Heidi of the Mountains.

"I can't right now," Lucy said. "But I'd like to later, maybe. Anyway, I came to give you one of these." She drew one of the invitation boxes out of her sack.

"What is it?" Betsy peeled off the thin layer of tape and slid the bottle out of the box. She uncorked the bottle and drew out the invitation.

"A party! All right!"

"Can you come?" Lucy spoke just a little too quickly. "I mean, you don't have to RSVP or anything. Just come if you can. I was just wondering, that's all."

"Sure, I wouldn't miss it," Betsy said. "I'll check with my mom. What can I buy for you?"

Buy for me?

"Oh!" Lucy's eyes widened. "A birthday present!"

Would everyone think they had to buy her a gift? She'd forgotten about that.

"It's a . . . uh, no-gift party," she said.

"Okay. Maybe I'll think of something little," Betsy said. She slid the invitation back in the bottle. "Can't wait!"

Lucy smiled and sighed and waved good-bye. As she backed down the steps, she consulted her folding map and strode through the tiny town. She didn't know too many of the other girls by name; she hoped she'd recognize them from the beach.

No one answered at the next house; she left the invitation propped against a sturdy wooden door with a fish skeleton scrolled on it.

At the third house, a mean dog barked and Lucy stayed on the sidewalk. Finally a man in an undershirt came out and took the invitation, promising to hand it right over to Lydia.

What am I doing? This is crazy, inviting people I don't even know to a party. She remembered Serena's happy face on the beach, planning their Diary Deed together. She thought about all those birthdays with no party. Then she took a deep breath and knocked on the fourth door.

"Hi!" she said when a slightly familiar girl opened the

door. "You might not remember me, but I'm Serena's friend."

So much for not relying on Serena, she thought with a wry smile.

"I remember you from the beach," the girl said.

Lucy looked at the addressed box. *Erica.*

"Well, I'm having a birthday party on Friday night. Since I'm going to be living here this summer, I thought I'd invite some people. You don't have to bring a present, though. And Serena will be there, too."

Did it sound as dumb from the other side as it did coming out of her mouth?

"I have something on Friday night, I think," Erica said. She didn't look too friendly.

"Okay," Lucy said, her heart sinking. "Come if you can."

As she walked around the corner toward the next address, Lucy wiped the sweat from the back of her neck again. She noticed the missing beaded necklace. Her neck felt lonely without it.

She gave the fifth invitation to a big brother, then knocked on the door of the sixth girl.

After Lucy told her about the party, and that Serena would be there, the girl said something strangely familiar.

"Okay," Amy said. "I . . . I think I have something on Friday night, though, so I'll have to check. Okay?"

"Okay, just come if you can. Don't bring a present, though." Lucy headed toward the street. "Two people said the same thing! Either people have plans or they're just making it up so they don't have to say no," she muttered to herself. Erica hadn't looked too friendly, but Amy did. Lucy peeked into her bag. Two invitations left.

As she rounded the corner, she arrived at Sweet Dreams. The store sold candy and soda and ice cream. Lucy checked her hair in the window before going in and made sure her pearl-pink nails still looked good.

Jake worked behind the counter. His family owned the store. She read the counter sign while she waited for him to ring up a customer.

"Hi, Dr Pepper," Jake called out as he finished with the customer. Lucy grew warm, remembering how they'd met last week when Serena had shown Lucy around and Lucy had ordered Dr Pepper from the store. They'd met again on the lawn of the church up the street, too, but by accident.

"I mean Lucy, right?" he said.

She smiled. "Lucy. Right."

Why was she here? She could buy candy anywhere in town!

"What's in the bag?" he asked, peeking over the counter top.

"Party invitations. Well, my birthday is Friday, and Serena wanted to have a party. It's going to be at my dad's office so all the girls could come. It's on Sunset Street. A big brown-and-white house."

Why am I spilling my guts?

"Happy birthday!" Jake said. "If I remember right, you hate ice cream?"

Lucy nodded.

"Can I get you a Dr Pepper, then?" he asked politely.

"No. But . . . ah, do you sell Jelly Bellies?"

"We're getting a shipment later this week, but we're out right now," Jake said. "Sorry."

"Thanks anyway," Lucy said. Someone else helped the new customers, but there wasn't much else to say. "Bye!" she said. The doorbell cheered as she left.

Bad move. I looked extremely dumb and still didn't get any Jelly Bellies.

Two invitations left: Jenny's and Julie's. Lucy didn't know where Jenny lived; maybe Lucy's dad could help.

Julie, well . . .

Maybe it was time for a break.

Two stores down was Dove Books and Gifts, so Lucy stepped in to cool off in the air-conditioned store. She still felt like an alien in the Christian store. She'd hardly ever been in one; just last week, Claudette had brought her in there.

After browsing for a few minutes, Lucy saw a display of cool wire necklaces: *Wired for Christ*, the display said. The necklaces were smooth silver spiral chains, each with a cross dangling just at heart level. Lucy held it against her chest and looked into the display mirror. If she wore it, it would just about cross her heart. . . .

Maybe she'd feel closer to Him if He were closer to her. She felt closer just warming the necklace in her hand.

She grabbed the two that were left.

One for Serena. I'll give it to her the night of our party, and we'll wear them together.

After paying, she glanced at her watch. "Better get Claudette. Pedal boating."

Lucy tossed her wallet and her purchases into the nearly empty beach bag. The last two invitations were down there, too, in the sunken pit of the bottom of the bag.

Lucy picked up Claudette at her house, and the two of them walked to the pedal boats. Lucy fastened a life jacket first around Claudette and then herself.

"This is great!" Claudette said. She threw some pieces of popcorn at the fish; they had bought a bag on the pier. "Here, fishy-fishy."

"It's great, isn't it?" Lucy said. The sun felt good on her hair, and the two of them circled and giggled around the port. After an hour pedaling around the harbor, they checked their boat back in.

"Thanks, Lucy!" Claudette hugged her.

Lucy hugged her back.

"Can we stop on the way home and get some science gum?" Claudette asked. They clomped across the wooden planks of the Green Pleasure Pier toward the streets of Avalon.

"Science gum?" Lucy asked. "Do they sell it at Von's Grocery Store?"

"Of course, silly. They sell it everywhere."

Lucy looked puzzled. "I don't get it."

"Experiment gum," Claudette said impatiently.

"I'll take you, even though I don't know what it is." A few blocks later they walked into the ministore, past the rows of neat apples and soft bread that had to be barged to the Island twice a week. Living on an island meant that if the sea was rough, no barge came.

Claudette pulled her into the candy row and held up a white pack of gum.

Lucy giggled. "*Now* I see what you mean. Spearmint gum, Claudette. It's not experiment gum." She reached into her beach bag for her wallet. "I can tell your dad is a scientist."

"I know it's really spearmint," Claudette teased. "But I didn't when I was little."

Lucy smiled. Claudette was smart. Really smart. But she wouldn't be eight years old till the end of the summer, so she still seemed little to Lucy.

"Lucy!" Claudette whispered loudly. "Look at that lady! Her skin looks green!" Lucy looked up and saw Claudette pointing at a woman with too much yellowish makeup on her face, not applied very neatly.

"Shh," Lucy whispered back.

Just then that same woman came all the way around the narrow isle, pushing her clackety cart. Someone was with her. Someone with a long brown ponytail that swung as she walked. Someone who probably had heard Claudette.

It was a small island, after all.

Here was Julie.

Purple Means Worry

Monday afternoon and evening . . .

Oh man. That must be Julie's mom. Had Julie actually heard Claudette?

"Look," Claudette raised her voice, pointing right at Julie. "Isn't that one of Serena's friends? Didn't we sit on the beach with her last week?"

"Claudette, don't point!" Lucy whispered.

Julie's mom gunned the grocery cart right past Lucy and around the corner, stopping at the next row. Lucy glanced into her cart. Three tiny apples, a pack of cheap computer paper, a carton of cigarettes.

Julie stopped right in front of Lucy. She didn't speak.

"Hi, Julie," Lucy said.

"Hi."

Julie didn't say anything about green skin. *Whew.* Lucy

twisted the strings from her beach bag around her hand until the blood was almost cut off, then untwisted them. They left red marks on her skin.

Lucy opened up the bag.

"Serena and I are having a party this week, for my birthday." She handed over the box addressed to Julie. "Here's an invitation."

Julie turned the box in her hands, examining it from all angles, then launched it toward her mother's cart a few feet away. It landed with a thud.

"Well, I'll be seeing you," Lucy said, walking slowly backward and keeping her eyes to the side, like you would move away from a strange dog.

"Later," Julie agreed. She joined her mom in the next aisle.

Through the thin rows of crackers and cookies, Lucy could hear Julie talking with her mom. Her voice sounded different. Like a little girl's.

"Can I please have a new brush?" she pleaded with her mother. "Mine has holes in it where the bristles fell out, and it's hard to use. They're only five dollars."

"I don't have five dollars," her mother barked.

Lucy and Claudette paid for the spearmint gum and left the store.

"She was mean," Claudette said as the bright sun kissed their skin, bringing warmth to the surface.

"Who, Julie or her mom?"

"Both," Claudette answered. Lucy nodded.

"Are you going to be home tomorrow morning?" Claudette asked. "I'm coming over with my mom. I could show you my new jump rope song."

"I'm going to be with Serena all day tomorrow," Lucy answered.

"Oh. All day. Again." Claudette's face fell.

Lucy nodded gently. "Here we are at your house." Lucy shooed Claudette toward her front door. "See you later!"

"Bye," Claudette called back as her mother opened the door and handed some money to Lucy, which Lucy refused.

"I don't mind you paying me for baby-sitting, but this time I told Claudette I'd take her pedal boating instead of her coming to my party," Lucy said. She waved good-bye and headed the few blocks back to her own home.

She walked into the kitchen and took the bowl of egg salad out of the refrigerator.

"Get them all delivered?" her mom called from the laundry room.

"Almost all. Except one. Dad has to help me find the address." Most people in Avalon lived within a few blocks of Lucy's house. Jenny's street wasn't on her small map, though.

Lucy smeared egg salad over a piece of toast and gulped a glass of milk. Then she went upstairs. It had been a long time since she'd taken a nap. Today she needed one.

🐜 🐜 🐜

"Serena called while you were sleeping this afternoon," her dad told her as Lucy curled up in a chair and read that evening. "I'm sorry I forgot. I had quite a few calls and got caught up in work."

"Dad!" Lucy looked at her watch. She could still call. In half an hour it would be nine o'clock, and Lucy wasn't allowed to call friends after that.

"Did she say what it was about?"

"No," her father sighed. "But she did say it was important. I'm sorry, Sparky. I should have written it down."

Lucy stomped upstairs. Imagine the trouble around here if *she* had forgotten to give *him* a message.

She dialed Serena's number. No answer. She hung up the phone and looked out her back window. Serena lived kitty-corner from her, behind and over one house. She could see the light on in Serena's room, the filmy curtain clouding the light in Serena's attic bedroom to milky white.

Lights were on. So they must be home.

Lucy dialed again. No answer. After about ten rings, the voice mail came on. Lucy left a message and then hung up.

She knew what was happening. Roberto, Serena's older brother, was on the phone. He never answered call-waiting.

Lucy twisted her mood ring. It was throbbing red. Anger ran through her arms and chest.

Why did everyone think her messages were unimportant? What if Julie had called Serena? What if Serena had to change their plans for tomorrow? Why didn't Roberto answer the phone if he was going to hog it all night?

Hey! An idea popped into Lucy's mind. She ran over and turned her bedroom lights on and off, fast, about ten times. Then she ran to the window to see if Serena had been watching, catching the signal. Nothing. She waited five more minutes, then tried again.

She blinked the lights on and off again ten more times and raced to the window once more, peering out into the dusk. She stared at Serena's milky white curtain, but no one peeked through them.

Then the doorbell rang! She looked at her watch. Ten till nine. Could it be Serena? Could she have made it over here that fast?

Lucy hung out at the top of the stairs and watched while her dad opened the door and talked in a low voice. Then he closed the door.

"Lucy?" he called out. Lucy ran down the stairs.

"Is that Serena?" she asked, looking toward the door. "Is she on the porch?"

"No," her dad said. "It's the next-door neighbor. He was outside with his little boy and saw your lights blinking on and off. His little boy was worried and wanted to make sure we're okay. We are okay, aren't we?"

Lucy covered her face with her hands. *Oh man!* "Yes, I'm fine. I was hoping Serena would see the lights. Don't worry." She walked upstairs. One minute till nine.

She dialed Serena's number once again, hoping for an answer. Ten rings, no answer. This time she didn't leave a message.

She hung up the phone and sat on her bed, alone.

"I'm nervous." The sound of her own voice in the quiet room surprised her.

She glanced at the CD player, then slipped in one of the Christian CDs Serena had loaned her. It was good music. Funny how such a simple thing made her feel better, nearer to God.

Lucy lay tummy-down on her bed, legs bent at the knees, toes pointing toward heaven. *What* important thing had Serena called about?

Lucy's hands cooled and her mood ring turned purple.

There was nothing she could do now. She'd have to wait till tomorrow to figure it out.

Oh No!

Tuesday morning . . . D Day minus three

"Mom?" Lucy poked her head into the living room, where her mother was painting.

"Yes?" Mom answered in the tight voice she used when interrupted. "I've got to finish this before Grace Kingsley and Claudette get here this morning."

Lucy swallowed back her anger. Sometimes it felt as if painting were more important than she was! "I'm going to Serena's, and then the beach, probably for the day." Lucy stepped into the room. "Is that still okay?"

"What about lunch?" her mother asked.

"We're going to pack a lunch at her house and bring it with us." Lucy sat down on the swivel chair behind her mother's desk. She picked her feet up and spun around and around. Then she stopped.

"Mom, can I buy something from you?" she asked, scanning the stacks on her mother's desk.

Mom set her brush down. "What?"

"Can I buy one of these?" Lucy held up one of the new leather sketch pads.

"You don't have to buy it from me," her mother said. "I'd be glad if you wanted to draw."

"I hate to disappoint you, but it's not for me," Lucy said.

"Ah." Her mother turned back to her half-empty canvas. "Serena."

"Can I still have one? I'll do some extra jobs to make up for it."

Her mother nodded absentmindedly. Lucy opened up the desk drawer and took out some high-quality pencils. After writing in the new book for a minute, she snapped it shut.

"I'll see you later." Lucy worked the sketch pad into the bottom of her beach bag and headed toward Serena's house.

Her tummy twisted. What had Serena been calling about yesterday? Something important!

Cloud after cloud thickened the sky, bouncing together and then scattering, like bumper cars. The sea breeze grew up to be a sea wind. A few minutes later Lucy knocked at the door, and Serena opened it up.

"Come upstairs," she said. "Quick!"

Lucy ran up the stairs, following Serena into her room. Serena's gray cat, Putty, licked her paws from a pillow on the yellow-checked bed. Lucy sat down next to him.

"Big trouble," Serena said. She grabbed a card off of her desk and handed it to Lucy.

"My brother Roberto went to get the mail yesterday;

we only pick it up about once a week. Look what was in there!"

Lucy opened the card and read: *You are invited to a birthday party for Jenny. Please come next Friday night, 7:00* P.M.

"Oh no!" Lucy said. "Friday night! I thought she already *had* her birthday."

"I tried to call you," Serena said, "but you didn't call me back!"

"Believe me, I tried," Lucy said, kicking off her flower-powers and crossing her legs as she scanned the invitation again.

"So what did Jenny say when you delivered her invitation yesterday?" Serena asked.

Lucy's stomach dropped. "The only one I couldn't deliver was Jenny's. I didn't know where she lived."

Serena groaned. "So now she'll think—"

"That I didn't invite her on purpose!" Lucy finished. "That I'm trying to have a birthday party competition with her or something." She slid onto the floor. "Now I know why Erica and Amy said they thought they might have plans. They just didn't want to tell me *what* plans."

"And I'm sure Jenny didn't invite you because you only got here and she didn't really know you," Serena explained. "She's nice. She wouldn't leave you out."

"No," Lucy said. "But she's going to think I left *her* out. In fact, everyone will think that. That I'm trying to overtake her party. Should I call her and explain?"

Serena headed toward the door. "We're sure to see some

of them at the beach today. I'll help you explain if you want!"

Lucy nodded, her stomach feeling like it did the night she accidentally gulped milk that had been sitting on the counter since breakfast.

"Let's go make lunch," Serena said.

Lucy caught a peek of Roberto watching music TV in the family room. Serena took some tortillas from the cupboard. "Do you want a burrito?" she asked Lucy.

"Mmmm," Lucy answered. She spied the TV remote control on the counter, and a funny memory perked her up.

"One time I played a trick on my dad," she whispered. "I got out of sight and turned the channel on the TV with the remote. He thought something was wrong with the TV and kept trying to fix it. I let it sit there for a while, then changed it again."

Serena grinned. "Give me that remote!"

The two of them tiptoed around the corner, Lucy stationed where she could see Roberto, Serena where the remote would work best. Serena changed the channel to Kiddie Cartoons.

"What?" Roberto said. He looked for the remote, then finally got up and changed the TV back to the music. He sat back down, picked up his guitar, and started to strum along.

Lucy counted to ten and signaled to Serena again. On came cartoons.

"What is going on?" Roberto stood up again, set down

his guitar, and banged the TV. Then he changed the channel again.

As soon as he sat down, Lucy gave the signal. Back on cartoons. This time, both girls laughed.

"Serena! *Eres un gorro!* You're an airhead!" He stormed past Lucy and into the kitchen. "Why don't you get serious about something for a change. I'm trying to practice my music!" He grabbed a tortilla and folded it before taking a bite. Then he grabbed the remote control and headed back into the family room, where he slammed the door.

"Brothers," Serena said, shaking her head. "No sense of humor."

But Lucy saw the hurt shadow Serena's eyes. "I'm sorry I caused a problem."

"It's all right," Serena said. "It's just big brothers. He is always playing jokes on my friends and me. Like last year at my birthday party. He thinks he's better than me. Smarter. Cuter. More Mexican, like our dad."

Lucy's eyes shadowed with her own hurt. "I wouldn't mind, if only I had a brother to celebrate my birthdays with. Or a sister. Either would have been fine," she whispered.

Serena looked surprised.

Lucy abruptly looked at the counter top. "Thanks for bringing lunch. I'll bring it next time."

"*De nada,*" Serena said. "Let's go get the umbrella and my beach bag."

"Do you think we'll need the umbrella?" Lucy asked. "It's a little cloudy."

Serena agreed. She walked up the stairs, more slowly

now. Once they got to her room, Lucy patted the bed next to her.

"I have something for you."

"What?" Serena sat down.

Lucy dug into her beach bag, past Jenny's invitation, and pulled out the sketchbook. "No more scraps of paper," she said. She presented it with flourish to Serena. "For you!"

Serena took it in both hands. "For me? I can't pay for it, though."

"It's a *gift*, silly," Lucy said. "No more scraps of paper in the garbage, okay?" She pretended to grumble. "I don't know why God surrounds me with all these artsy types."

Serena hugged her before opening the book. A tear filled the corner of her eye as she read what Lucy had written: *To Serena, a friend of faith, and my Faithful Friend. Lucy.*

"I believe in you, and in your art," Lucy said to her.

Serena nodded and set the sketchbook on her dresser top. "No more scraps," she promised. "Thank you so much."

"De nada," Lucy repeated what Serena had said minutes before, and they laughed together.

Lucy stood and picked up her beach bag—with Jenny's lonely invitation floating near the top.

"And now, rain or shine, trouble or not, I guess it's off to the beach."

Unwelcome Message

By the time the girls got to the beach, it was blowing harder. They scanned the sand but didn't see anyone they knew. A man was screaming into the pay phone right behind their usual beach spot.

"Let's go behind the Casino instead," Serena said, referring to the big domed auditorium that held the movie theater and island ballroom. The movie theater had one thousand red velvet seats, and the walls were decorated with tile paintings. Lucy had peeked in once but had never gone inside. "The scuba dive park is there, and it's out of the wind a bit. Maybe the others are there."

They trudged over and sat down on the sand. There were a handful of tourist families and a couple of towels nearby where the scuba divers had set their gear. No one they knew was parked on the sand, though.

"Okay, time for party plans. Want to plan the food?" Serena asked. "I feel like I'm not doing enough to help with the party."

"I'm sorry," Lucy said. "I hope my family hasn't taken over!"

"No, no," Serena said.

Lucy thought she looked sad. "Why don't we write down the food together, and then *you* can do all the music yourself? You're so good with music."

Serena beamed. They unwrapped their burritos and ate and chattered.

Lucy wrote down what they decided on. *Burgers, chips, watermelon, birthday cake. Dr Pepper.*

Serena looked over her shoulder. "Maybe you should get some other kinds of soda, too."

"You think?" Lucy teased. She jotted down, *7-Up, Coke, Diet.*

"A birthday cake! You'd better order it soon or there won't be time."

"Where?" Lucy asked.

Serena jotted down an address on her napkin. "It's a little out of the way, but if you leave from Jenny's house, you'll be closer."

"Jenny's house?" Lucy's voice filtered into the breeze.

"You've got to stop by with her invitation on the way home, right? I'd go with you"—Serena checked her watch—"but when I told my mom we were leaving, she said I have to be home in an hour to help her clean up." Serena tossed her empty napkin into her beach bag.

"Oh. I thought we were going to spend the whole day together." Lucy folded her napkin around the uneaten half of her burrito and slipped it into her bag. She twisted her silver ring.

"Me too," Serena said. "I'm sorry!"

Just then, two guys in gear surfaced in the scuba park in front of them.

"Look! It's my friend Philip!" Serena said. "And his dad." She fixed her hair a bit and tucked in her shirt.

"How can you tell?" Lucy asked, staring at the two strange men in black diving gear.

"His suit." Serena pointed out the large octopus on his wet suit. The boy and man approached the beach.

Philip came closer and waved. "Hi, Serena."

"This is my friend Lucy," Serena said.

"Nice to meet you." Philip smiled at Lucy. She smiled back.

Philip reached into his bag and took out a Polaroid camera. He handed it to Serena. "Would you take a picture of me and my dad in our gear?"

"Sure," Serena said. She snapped a picture and handed it, with the camera, back to him.

"Will you take our picture, too?" Serena asked. "I'll pay you back for the film."

"No problem." Philip snapped a picture of Lucy and Serena on the beach, arm in arm. He handed the copy to Serena.

After a minute of small talk, the two of them left.

"We'd better get going, too," Serena said. "It's too windy for me, and you've got work to do."

"Right-o," Lucy said, wishing she could just go home and play the piano or read instead of trying to make a lame explanation to Jenny.

They picked up their gear and parted a block later, Serena turning right to go home, Lucy left to head toward Jenny's.

As she approached Jenny's street, Lucy slowed down. By the time she got to Jenny's house, she was practically a snail with a broken foot.

Lucy checked the street address on the invitation box with the one on the house in front of her. It was the right house.

Mama mia. Serena shoulda been here.

As Lucy walked up the steps, she heard crying through an open upstairs window. It wasn't loud, but it was definitely noticeable. It sounded like a girl. Maybe a twelve-year-old girl.

Oh no! Maybe I should leave! But what if someone has seen me hanging out here?

Lucy knocked lightly on the door. The crying abruptly stopped. Lucy knocked again, but no one answered.

Too strange! Lucy left the box with the invitation near the door and left the house with long, quick steps.

Once down the street, she radioed her mother on her two-way radio.

"Mom?"

"Yes, hi, Lucy. How is your day so far, honey?"

"Good!" Lucy said. "Serena told me about a bakery. I was going to, well, order a birthday cake. Unless you wanted to bake one or already ordered one," she ended hopefully.

"No, I'm sorry. I'll bake you one if you want," her mother said. "I've never done it. I can't guarantee the results, but maybe it will turn out okay. A first time for everything!"

Oh great. A flat party and a flat cake.

"No, that's okay, Mom. I'll just order it myself," Lucy said. "Be home in half an hour or so." Lucy waited till the golf cart traffic went by and crossed the street. Few cars were allowed on Catalina Island, but the place swarmed with golf-carted go-getters scooting around.

Why do I feel so sad? I told Dad I wanted to plan this myself.

Lucy walked a ways, then stepped into the sweet-smelling shop and ate a bagel. She ordered a plain white cake to be picked up Friday. Then she took the long way home.

As she walked up to her front porch, she saw something glittering in the jasmine bush to the right of the door. She stooped down and saw what it was—a bottle. One of the bottles she had sent her invitations in.

Inside was a scrap of paper. Lucy shook the bottle till the paper fell out into her hand. She unfolded it and saw a neatly typed message on plain computer paper. It said, *Stop the Party!*

Lucy's head felt light, and she sat down on the front step with her head in her hands, letting the paper flutter to the ground.

Do You Belong?

Lucy woke up exhausted. Through the entire night she'd wrestled with the idea that she should tell someone about the note. Her mom and dad would definitely over-react to trouble. Besides, she'd always handled things on her own, right?

Who had sent it? Jenny would have had time to run it over, if she'd hurried. Or had Julie cooked up something new?

And what if it *was* Jenny? After all, it was a big mix-up and not really Lucy's fault. Maybe Lucy should call her and explain about the party.

After breakfast, Lucy picked up the telephone to call Serena. She could ask Serena for Jenny's number since she couldn't remember her last name.

Lucy hung the phone up again. If she did that, she'd have to tell Serena why she wanted the number right now. And then Lucy would *have* to tell Serena what she was planning to do—offer to cancel the party. Lucy didn't want to hurt Serena's feelings about their diary plan. They could figure something else out if they had to. But Lucy had to do the right thing.

So Lucy stuck the slam note into one pocket and grabbed her Jelly Belly case. Before putting it into her other pocket, she snagged a couple of Cafe Latte jelly beans to cheer herself up. Then she headed out the door.

Heat already rose from the paved streets, mixing with the salt air into a clammy-smelling brew. No new rain today, just a steamy aftertaste from yesterday's rain. Lucy's sandals flip-flopped up the street, snapping with each step. Around the corner, she passed . . . that church.

Last week she'd watched Jake plant flowers outside the old white church, neatly tended by the Islanders for more than one hundred years. It had been a long time since she'd been in a church. Lucy had just told that to Serena, hadn't she? She felt the hate note in her pocket. Maybe now was the time to go.

She turned around and walked more slowly, her sandals quieting to little cricket-like chirps. As she approached the church, Lucy saw that the door was open.

She stood outside the neatly painted doorway for a minute, hoping somehow she'd know what to do. Inside, the wooden pews gleamed, and the forest green carpet seemed newly vacuumed. Lucy took two small pieces of paper that talked about the church from the information booth and slipped them into her back pocket.

She tiptoed in and sat in the seat nearest to the door, setting her Jelly Belly case next to her, since it pinched in her pocket when she sat down.

She looked around. *I forget what to do in a church.*

She reached in front of her and touched the Bible that was stuck into the wooden rail attached to the pew in front of her.

"Excuse me!" came a voice from in front.

Lucy jumped up, her Jelly Belly case clattering to the floor. "Me?" she asked.

"I'm sorry to have startled you." A teenaged girl stepped from a room just to the side of the altar in front of the church. "Do you belong here?"

Lucy bent down and collected her case, then slipped out of the pew. "No, I'm sorry. I guess I don't belong here at all."

The girl waved her hand. "No! That's not what I mean. I meant, do you belong to this church? Do you go here? It's just that I've never seen you."

"Oh." Lucy sat down, perching at the edge of the pew again. "No, I guess I'm just here, uh, looking."

"My name is Rachel. I work at the Christian camp on the Island, but I'm in Avalon for the day helping out around here." She pointed to the vacuum cleaner. "Slave labor, you know."

"Oh." Lucy didn't know what else to say.

"I'll be around if you have any questions." Rachel slipped into the side room again.

Then she stepped back out for a second. "And if you're looking, then this *is* the place you belong." She smiled at Lucy, who shyly smiled back.

Lucy scooted over in the pew again. In front of her was

a brass plate tacked in between the Bible holders. It read, *In memory of Marion Davidson*. She scooted over and read the next one: *I am the Way, the Truth, and the Life.*

She looked toward the altar again and closed her eyes.

Jesus, it's getting a little messy around here. I have this note, you see, and I am afraid. Also, I'm not really feeling like I belong.

"If you're looking, then this is the place you belong," came silently back to Lucy's heart.

Lucy opened her eyes and saw the stained-glass portrait of Jesus to the left of the cross up front. The light outdoors streamed through the blend of colored glass, the sun bringing the picture to life. On Jesus' lap were little children. His arms snuggled around them, pulling them close.

Lucy stood up and tried to move forward to look more closely. Only her feet wouldn't move. Her legs didn't want to go even though she wished they would. Her hands shook.

"I'm sorry," she whispered into the stillness. "I'm still not sure what to do."

She hung out for a minute, hoping Rachel would come back. She didn't know what to say if she did. She just wanted to see her again. But Rachel was gone.

Lucy turned around and walked slowly out into the daylight again. "Guess I'd better get on to Jenny's."

Down the block and to the left. A few blocks over. Jenny's house.

Lucy stood in the exact same spot she had yesterday. She rang the doorbell. This time, Jenny answered.

"Hi," Lucy started. "I'm Lucy."

Of course I'm Lucy, she said to herself inside her head. *I'm certainly not the mailman, not in this town.*

"I, uh, left you an invitation to my party yesterday."

Jenny looked back. Her eyes were ringed, and she had one tooth that stuck out between her lips just a little, like the little tooth a baby bird uses to peck out of its egg. "I know."

"Well, I just wanted to tell you that I had *no* idea that you were having a party that day. I thought you might be mad about it."

Mad enough to write a mean note, she wanted to add. But didn't.

Jenny looked at her and said nothing.

Lucy swallowed. "I'm really sorry for any hurt I caused. I'm going to cancel my party so that there's no competition."

Jenny smiled. "That's really nice of you. But my party has to be cancelled anyway."

"What?" Lucy asked.

"My grandpa is sick. We just found out yesterday how sick. He lives with us, so I can't have kids over here." Her smile hid again.

Lucy's heart hurt for Jenny. "Oh, well, I'm really sorry."

Suddenly Lucy had a great idea! "Jenny, if you want to, you can have your party with me. On Friday night. We could do it together!"

Jenny looked startled.

"It's going to be where my dad works, and it's a big place. So everyone could come."

"Well . . ." Jenny struggled. "Thanks, but . . . ah, I hardly know you."

"That's okay," Lucy said. "The address is on the invitation. You could bring anyone you want," she said.

"I probably invited the same kids you did," Jenny said. "There aren't too many girls our age on the Island. My mom doesn't know you, either. She wouldn't feel comfortable."

"Your mom can come, too," Lucy said.

"My mom went over town to get oxygen and some special medications for my grandpa. She won't be home till Friday. Besides"—Jenny looked at her hands—"Julie said if I went to your party, she wouldn't be my friend anymore."

Lucy held her breath and opened her eyes wide. "Did she tell *everyone* that?" she finally asked.

Jenny shrugged; the rings around her eyes grew darker.

"I can't do anything about that." Lucy's chest hurt. "But you're still welcome to come. And anyone else you want to come, your mom, too. We can celebrate together."

Jenny nodded, but she still looked doubtful.

Lucy waved weakly and left, flip-flopping toward her house as fast as she could.

You know, this has gone far enough. Maybe I did something to hurt Julie, maybe not. But I think it's time to find out.

"Hi, Mom." Lucy walked in the house and looked at the list of names, phone numbers, and addresses Serena had brought over to address the invitations last Sunday night. They'd stuck it to the refrigerator door with a magnet after

they were finished. Julie's last name must be on there somewhere.

"Whatcha doing?" her mother asked.

"Looking for a phone number. Oh, by the way, I invited this girl Jenny"—Lucy tapped Jenny's name on the
list on the refrigerator—"to share the birthday party with
me if she wants. Hers got cancelled because her grandpa is
sick. She said she'd ask her mom. She didn't look too sure
about it." Lucy copied Julie's number onto her hand and
frowned. "How sad for her. No party."

"Jenny, huh?" her mom said. "That was sweet of you."

Lucy nodded and hurried up to her room. When she
got there, she closed the door and dialed the phone.

"May I speak with Julie?"

"This is Julie."

"Hello. This is Lucy Larson, Serena's friend."

"The new girl," Julie said. "What do you want?"

"Have I hurt your feelings in some way or done something wrong to you?"

"Why would you think that?" Julie said in a singsong
voice.

"It just seems like you really don't like me."

"Good guess," Julie said.

Lucy took a deep breath. "Did you tell other people not
to come to my party?"

"What's it to you?"

Lucy didn't know what to answer. Finally she sputtered
out, "You know, you're really mean. Saying mean things,
doing mean things, writing slam notes in people's invitations and putting them at their house. MEAN!"

"Slam notes in invitations?" Julie said. "You're crazy. Really crazy."

The other line clicked off, and soon a dial tone came on. Julie had hung up.

For a moment a wisp of doubt crossed Lucy's mind. Had Julie written the note? She must have. Who else would have?

A hot tear ran down Lucy's cheek. She flopped on her bed and stuffed her face into her pillow and cried. Why did *she* have to do all the work making friends? Couldn't anyone else make a try, too? It seemed that if she wanted friends, she had to make the moves. It was too hard. And right now, it didn't seem worth it at all.

After she stopped sniffling, Lucy realized she'd have to call Serena and tell her it was very likely no one was coming to their party at all. So much for their exciting summer. And that they'd have to write total and complete *failure* as the first entry in their own summer diary.

Maybe with such a terrible beginning Serena wouldn't think that their summer diary adventures looked fun at all. Or worth doing together anymore.

10

Countdown

Even though the party might be a failure, Lucy and Serena were still friends. And that felt good.

"Plug your nose!" Lucy called as Serena cannonballed off of the boat. The white boat rocked like a cradle with the force of the jump. Lucy giggled as Serena surfaced and swam next to her.

The sun beamed down on Lucy's shoulders, warming her from the outside in. This day was shaping up much, much better than the day before.

Even though nothing had changed, really.

"Let's snorkel!" Lucy suggested next. She swam up to the boat and called, "Dad! Toss us the masks and the snorkel gear!"

Her dad threw two masks and breathing tubes into the water. "Not more than twenty feet from the boat," he warned, and Lucy nodded.

She slipped her mask on and so did Serena.

"I'm glad no one else is here to see us look like this," Lucy said.

"Anyone in particular?" Serena teased. Lucy laughed back.

They took their kickboards and placed them under their tummies, then floated a bit away from the boat. The cool blue water lapped at Lucy's skin, refreshing and soothing at the same time. Something brushed her leg, and she turned just in time to see it.

Her eyes opened wide, and she paddled closer to Serena and pointed. Lucy pulled the breathing tube out of her mouth. "Garibaldi!" she said, pointing at the rare orange creatures, piloting by like overgrown goldfish. It was a strange sensation—ticklish and weird at the same time, rubbing up against fish.

Serena nodded and pointed. A school of baby top smelt swam by, their silvery skin flashing through the water like dimes falling to the sea floor.

"Aah! A rock shark!" Serena called out and the two girls paddled for their lives to the boat.

They climbed in, giggling.

"That didn't look like a shark!" Lucy said. "It was only ten inches long."

"I know. They're probably harmless," Serena laughed. "Let's lie out in the sun and warm up," she suggested, her teeth clacking behind pale lips.

Lucy nodded, and they headed toward the stern of the boat. "I'm glad your mom could come," she said, laying a huge, pineapple-colored towel on the platform and then settling on top of it.

"It was sweet of your mom to ask her," Serena said. "I hope they're getting along okay."

Lucy cocked her head at the sound of some female laughter from the boat's bow. "It sounds okay to me," she said. "My mom thought if we're going to spend so much time together, they should get to know one another. I wish your dad could have come, too."

"My dad works and stays in L.A. all week," Serena answered. "He's only on Catalina on the weekends." Serena spread her towel out, too, and in a flash the two were warm. "Did you bring your new diary?" she asked.

"*Our* diary now," Lucy said. She opened up the diary Grammy had sent her to record all of her summer adventures. When Lucy and Serena had decided to read the old diary together, they also agreed to write together in a new one.

"What should we write? I mean, we don't even know what's going to happen yet," Serena said.

"I can make an educated guess, and I'm not even a scientist," Lucy said. "The party will go bust."

"Don't say that. You don't know for sure if Julie talked with everyone. Do you want me to ask some people?"

"No, no, I don't want to make a big deal about it if she only said something to Jenny," Lucy said. "People will wonder why you're asking. I could make a huge problem where there might not be one. And if they say yes, then I don't know what to do anyway. I don't want to cause a big war."

"Okay, but I'll help however you want," Serena said.

"Thanks."

"And word will get around that you asked Jenny to

share your party, which was totally nice," Serena said. "Even though you won't know till the last minute since her mom is over town till tomorrow. Here, I'm dry now. Hand me that diary."

Lucy looked puzzled but handed it over—and stuck close enough to see over Serena's shoulder.

Serena took a pen from the nearby beach bag and wrote the date. *Dear Diary*, she wrote. *This is our new friendship diary, and I am going to tell you something really nice that Lucy did.*

Lucy dived for the pen, but Serena snatched her hand away just in time. "Nah," Serena said. "Remember, we said we are going to be totally honest and say whatever we want in here." She wrote down a few more things about their week and then doodled a picture of two girls with snorkel gear staring at a garibaldi. She handed the diary to Lucy.

"I think I'll write in it tomorrow night after the party," Lucy said. "I'll be honest, I promise. I'm just hoping for good news." Her voice softened. "What if the girls in the old diary had a party to die for and ours is a flop?"

A sad shade of gray passed over Serena's bright face. "Well, the results don't have to be the same," she said slowly.

I was hoping she'd say it for sure wouldn't be a bust, Lucy thought.

The two of them warmed in the sun till Lucy's dad pulled their boat, the *Gale Forces*, into port.

"Thank you so much," Mrs. Romero said as she and Serena left. "We had a wonderful time, and we'll have to have you over sometime soon."

Lucy looked pleased, as her mother and Serena's mother really seemed to like each other.

"Do you want me to help clean out the boat?" Lucy's mother asked as Lucy's dad tied the boat up.

"No thanks," he said.

"Then I think I'll head back and throw some laundry in."

"I'll stay with Dad, okay?" Lucy asked. Boating beat laundry by a backstroke any day.

"Sure," Mom said. "Anything you want me to make sure is clean for tomorrow night?"

Lucy's heart sped up. "I don't know. Capri pants, I guess," she said. "My Hawaiian shirt." *Hope that's not too islandy.*

Her mother waved and headed home.

"Ready for the big day, Sparky?" Dad said as he wound the rope around the berth.

"Yeah. I hope it's okay," Lucy answered. She hadn't mentioned the bottle and slam note. Or Julie. She drew the cord tight around the winches.

"Sure, it will be fine! We'll pick up the cake, the food, the music," her dad said. "My hula skirt."

"Dad!" Lucy protested. "Hey, can I walk down to the Shell Shack?" She pointed to the shop at the end of the dock.

"I'll meet you there as soon as I pump out the boat," her dad said. Lucy grabbed her shoulder bag and headed down the dock.

The shop was a little wooden hut with driftwood nailed all over it. Fishermen's nets covered the front, and one served as a screen door. Lucy pushed it aside and walked in.

"Can I help you?" A kindly older man with two missing teeth approached her.

"No, thank you," Lucy said.

She wandered the rows, admiring a shark-tooth necklace. Maybe she should buy one. But she'd just bought matching ones, special ones, for her and Serena.

The barrettes were cool, but her curls often covered them up.

On the last table in the back was a large abalone shell, split in half, and filled with anklets. The anklets were made out of tiny ivory puka shells. The sign said they were half price.

Lucy pulled out one after another, counting them as she did. Did she dare to buy them? They wouldn't take returns on sale items; the sign said so.

There were eleven anklets left. Lucy needed ten.

She gathered them up, leaving the abalone shell nearly empty, and brought them to the front of the store.

"I'd like all of these," she said softly.

The old man smiled, his teeth and gums stained brown with tobacco.

"A lot of friends, huh?" he said.

"I really don't know," Lucy said. He looked puzzled but wrapped them in a bag. Lucy paid and then stuck the purchase into her shoulder bag.

She walked out front and waited for her dad. A couple of boys shouted at the sea gulls, scaring them into the air. Lucy frowned at the young boys till they walked away, leaving the gulls alone. It was something she did a lot, even on the beach. She felt sorry for the gulls. Poor birds. They were *sea* gulls, after all. They had a right to be there.

"You ready?" her dad asked, walking up alongside her.

"I guess," Lucy answered.

🕯 🕯 🕯

That night after dinner, after kissing her mom and dad good-night, Lucy laid out her clothes. They were ironed, for once. She removed the chipped nail polish from her nails.

Shoulda had Serena paint them again, she thought.

She cleaned up her room and set the bag of anklets really close to her outfit.

Tomorrow she'd be twelve.

She put on her jammies, got into bed with her Tender Teddy, and thought about her last birthdays.

On Lucy's eleventh birthday, they had eaten moose meat in Alaska while her dad studied fern fronds with Claudette's dad. On her tenth birthday, they'd been in the Chilean rain forest studying vanishing tree species. On her ninth birthday, she'd had to stay with Grammy and Gramps. Gramps had played "The Birthday Song" on his accordion.

"I'm not unthankful, but this year I'd really like a birthday with lots of kids, Lord," Lucy whispered into the night. "A real kid party for once."

Lucy fell asleep with a smile, realizing that without even trying, she was beginning to pray on her own. She *was* growing closer to God.

This Is It!

Friday Morning . . . D Day!

Lucy woke early Friday morning to the sound of a bird chirping nonstop, like a smoke detector that needed its batteries replaced. She lay in bed with the window still open and thought . . .

I'm twelve.

With a smile on her face, Lucy stood and looked in the mirror. Her face looked the same. Maybe a little older.

Instead of putting on the clothes for the party, she tossed on some cutoff shorts and a T-shirt. She didn't want to get the party clothes dirty.

Then she walked downstairs to breakfast, taking dainty, ladylike steps on the way down.

Her dad had made cinnamon rolls; chubby raisins stuck like amber jewels into the frosted crown. They were hot. And he served her coffee.

"Coffee?" she wrinkled her nose.

"You're a young lady now." He bowed. Then he

whispered, "Don't worry, it's decaffeinated and has lots of sugar and cream."

Mom stepped into the room carrying a large box and a thin envelope. "Do you want your presents now or later?" She set the gifts on the table and kissed Lucy on the left cheek then, almost impulsively, smooched her on the right cheek, too.

"Now, of course!" Lucy said. "Why wait?"

She opened the big box first. Out came a light blue crepe dress, very mature looking and absolutely beautiful. "Wow, Mom." Lucy sucked in her breath. "I don't think you've ever bought something like this for me. Not since Uncle James' wedding, anyway."

"You're a lovely young lady. It will match your eyes," her mom said. "I sneaked away one morning and bought it."

I guess she's not always *painting,* Lucy thought with a pang of guilt.

At the bottom of the box were some strappy blue shoes with a little wedge heel and some sheer hose. Tied to the box ribbon was a bottle of pearl-pink polish.

"I thought it looked nice on you," her mom said. "I've never painted my nails myself, so I hope I got a good kind."

Lucy smiled. "I'm sure it will be great, Mommy."

She hadn't said Mommy for a long time. It felt good, rolling out of her heart and off of her tongue.

She sipped her coffee, pinky in the air, and took another bite of the soft roll.

Then Lucy opened the envelope. Inside was a one-hundred-dollar bill!

"Wow!" she said. "What's this for?"

"Your new dog," Dad said. "Your mom and I added a little extra this year, knowing what you're saving for. When we get back home at the end of the summer, we'll go to the pound and pick one out."

Lucy's eyes filled with tears. "This is the best ever."

"And now," Dad said, "let's go get the food for the party."

As her mom and dad went to grab their shoes and wallets, Lucy stuffed her mug into the top rack of the dishwasher and shut the door. She turned it on, and its low hum filled the room with vibrations. She met her parents at the door, and the three of them hopped into the golf cart and scooted off to Von's.

"We wrote out a whole list," Lucy said. Once at the store, they picked up burgers and buns with the fixings, chips and soda and watermelon.

"That's a lot of food," Lucy said, looking at it stack up in the cart.

"There will be a lot of hungry girls!" her mom said. "And I've never done this. Better too much than too little."

There may be way *too much*, Lucy thought. *Depending on who shows.*

She swallowed the thought and went to grab a couple of bags of ice and some tropical candles.

"Hey, look at these!" Dad showed up with an armful of pastel-colored Japanese lanterns. "We can string these around the patio. Fiesta!" He *cha-cha-cha*ed down the aisle.

Lucy's mom rolled her eyes. "I told you he was the party man."

Lucy giggled, glad that no one she knew was in Von's today.

They paid and then carted off down the street to pick up the cake. As they entered the bakery, warm, floury air tickled Lucy's nose and made her tummy rumble again, even though it hadn't been too long since the cinnamon rolls at home.

"Lucy," her mom said after the cashier opened the box for them to view the cake, "there's nothing written on this."

"I know," Lucy said. "I felt funny ordering 'Happy Birthday' to myself." She saw the pained look in her mom's eye. "It's okay. Plain white is fine. I don't want a fuss anyway."

Her mom nodded, silent. The two of them walked back outside. Lucy sat in the back of the golf cart, with the cake on her lap as her dad stuck the key into the ignition, and they took off.

Halfway home, he pulled over and hopped out at a flower stand.

"What's he doing?" Lucy asked. Mom shook her head as if to say, "I don't know."

Lucy watched as her dad swapped a ten-dollar bill for a sweet-smelling bunch wrapped in plastic and handed them to Lucy's mother.

So sweet. He bought flowers for her mom a lot lately.

When they got home and loaded the stuff into the house, Dad called Lucy into the kitchen.

He rummaged through the pantry till he found a vase,

then stuck the bouquet of flowers into it. *"Hibiscum a rosea."*

"English, please, Dad," Lucy said.

"Hibiscus. I always give flowers to people I love. These are for you."

Lucy reached a shaking hand over to take the vase.

Dad pulled one out and snapped off the stem. He stuck it behind her ear.

"You're a lovely young lady," he said. "I'm proud you're my daughter."

He's changing, Lucy noticed. *He's softer. Not as bossy. Maybe Jesus is changing him.* Her parents had committed their lives to Christ again only months before.

"Thanks, Dad." Lucy smooched him, then went upstairs, carrying her presents with her. She set them down on her dresser, then opened the pink nail polish and smoothed some over her nails, trying like anything to do it as well as Serena had.

Serena. Please don't let her down with this party.

Lucy remembered the Wired for Christ necklaces and fastened one around her neck. The cross hung right over her heart, where Jesus crossed her heart, sticking by her forever.

The second necklace she stuck into the pocket of her Capri pants, still neatly folded on her dresser top.

That was for Serena. Lucy'd bring it tonight.

Unfinished Business

Early Friday evening . . .

Lucy and her family took several treks in the golf cart in order to haul all of the party gear over to her dad's office. The patio was ready—thick-planked tables on one side for food, a small wicker table off to the other. Lucy arranged the puka shell anklets on top of the wicker table so they just looked like another decoration, and not what they really were—party gifts for girls who might not even come.

"Want to help me hang these lights up?" her dad asked. Lucy nodded, and they strung the Japanese lanterns from the whitewashed patio ceiling. The setting sunlight over the channel bronzed everything; reflections off of the water cast a glow across the patio. The room looked beautiful.

"Where should I put the food?" Serena asked, unpacking the plastic Von's bags.

"Let's set it all out except for the cake," Lucy said. "We can keep that in the back till it's time to light the candles."

"And make a wish!" Serena said. "Don't forget, you get to make a wish."

Lucy nodded her head slowly. "I think I know what I want to wish for. I just don't know right now if it can possibly come true."

Her dad looked at her but said nothing. He cut the watermelon in half for them, and Lucy scooped the fruit into balls while Serena cut the watermelon shell into a basket shape.

"Where did you get the pretty flowers?" Serena nodded toward the vase in the center of the food-serving table.

Lucy's ear tips turned pink. "They're from my dad. He says I'm a young lady now."

"Young laaaaaady," Serena teased, drawing out the word. "That explains the one behind the ear, then."

"Yeah, he put it there," Lucy said. "He said he always gives flowers to people he loves."

"Awww, sweet," Serena said. "Where was your mom off to in such a hurry?"

"Isn't she here?" Lucy looked around. She *hadn't* seen her in a long while.

"Nope. I saw her race off in a hurry in the golf cart like an hour and a half ago, just as I was coming here. She looked like her thoughts were a mile away."

"Oh," Lucy said. *What could be on her mind?*

"I think we're set up," Lucy's dad said. "I'm going to go home and rinse off. I'll be back in an hour or so, just before everyone arrives."

The girls nodded. Serena's brother fooled around on the back patio, setting up the stereo system for the girls.

"It's time, isn't it?" Serena asked. "Our first Diary Deed, copying what the girls did a long time ago. A terrific party. A beginning!"

Not an ending, I hope. Lucy swallowed.

As Serena leaned over to tie her shoe, Lucy noticed a thin chain with a cross on it dangling from her neck.

"I never noticed your necklace before," Lucy said. She thought about the Wired for Christ necklace in her pocket—the one she bought for Serena so they could wear them together.

"Oh yeah, I wouldn't be without it! My *abuela,* my grandma, gave it to me."

"Oh," Lucy said. The night wasn't starting as she had planned. Serena already had a necklace. Now she had nothing to give Serena to celebrate their first D Day.

Lucy's mouth got dry and her gum tasted stale all of a sudden. "I think I'll go throw this out," she said.

She stepped into the front room to collect her thoughts and lobbed her wad of gum toward the garbage can next to Mr. Kingsley's desk. It missed, so she knelt to pick up the gum and set it into the garbage can.

The garbage can overflowed with wadded-up papers, most of them with colored ink. *Claudette's computer games,* Lucy thought. One paper on top was almost open, and Lucy could read the word *Parte.*

She reached her hand toward the garbage can and took the paper out. She opened it up. It said *Stop the Parte.*

Stop the Parte. If it had been spell-checked, like Claudette had just been learning how to do, it would say *Stop the Party*.

Lucy's legs felt weak. Of course Claudette could have all the bottles she wanted, from the storeroom. And she'd visited Lucy's house on Tuesday.

Lucy sat on the floor, the rough carpet scratching against her legs, the beige walls spinning. *Claudette*.

She opened her eyes and looked toward the patio, which was cheery and bright, eager to enfold the party. The music sounded good. Serena was humming in the kitchen, ready to celebrate a birthday. Claudette had always celebrated with Lucy, too—moose meat in Alaska, a restaurant in Chile, or whatever. But not this year.

Claudette. *If Claudette did it, that means that Julie didn't write the note.*

Sadness, fear, and embarrassment filled Lucy's heart like a cup of water running over into the sink; it just kept coming and coming. She looked at her watch. She had to fix this, and she had to do it now!

"Will your brother stay with you till I come back?" she asked Serena.

"Yes, but where are you going?"

"I'll explain when I get back. I have to hurry so I get back before the party starts." *Even though I have no clue what I'm going to say*, she thought.

Serena nodded, and Lucy ran out the door and down the street, hoping like anything she didn't sweat up her party outfit.

Lord, I need some help. I need a few minutes to think this through, but I really don't have much time! People talked on cell phones while they jogged, others rode bikes, and noisy golf carts zipped by. Lucy couldn't keep her mind clear. *What should I say?*

A few blocks over, she turned to go down the street and caught sight of the white church on the green lawn. The yellow flowers Jake had planted last week winked and bloomed in the fading light. Lucy slowed to a walk.

I'll bet it's quiet in there. Quiet enough to think.

Lucy stepped into the church and this time sat toward the middle. The church was empty again, thankfully.

The lights were dim. She stared at the ceiling, sorting through all the things she could say to Claudette and Julie.

She glanced down. In front of her was another brass plate, fixed to the seat ahead of her, just like the others had been. This one said *Draw close to God, and He will draw close to you.*

Lucy closed her eyes.

I've been watching my mom and dad and Serena. I think I see how I might get close to you, God. Ask you into what I do, chat with you, tell you my dreams and fears. And, like right now, depend on you for help. I really need your help now!

Lucy stood up and walked toward the front of the church.

Just reach out and do it. Isn't that what Serena said?

The stained glass was darker than it had been the other day. Pale moonlight spilled through, though, illuminating Jesus' face.

This time, Lucy's feet moved forward when she told them to. She walked forward and stopped at the front. Then she reached up and slipped the flower from behind her ear and laid it on the ledge beneath the stained-glass picture of the Lord.

After a moment Lucy turned and walked out of the church. She checked her watch again. She had business to do, and very little time in which to do it.

Sisters

Friday evening . . .

After a few short blocks made quick with long steps, Lucy arrived at Claudette's house. A dim bulb flickered in a yellow bug glass outside the tidy front porch, though it was still twilight outside. Lucy took a deep breath, felt the crumpled-up note in her pocket, and knocked on the front door.

"Lucy!" Mrs. Kingsley answered the door. "Aren't you supposed to be at your party?"

"Yes," Lucy said. "In about half an hour or so. But there's something I need to talk about with you and Mr. Kingsley."

Mrs. Kingsley's eyes opened wide, and she ushered Lucy through the slender doorway.

"Is Claudette here?"

"She's up in her room." Mrs. Kingsley shut the door behind her and led Lucy to the living room. Unlike at Lucy's house, the people could actually *use* the furniture in this living room, Lucy noticed with a quick smile. Two lavender candles spread warmth and perfume through the air. Lucy balanced on a neat couch in the center of the room, and crossed her legs in a new, young ladylike manner. Claudette's dad joined them.

"I found a note on my doorstep a few days ago, and it said to stop the party," Lucy explained. "I wasn't sure who had sent it, but it was in one of the bottles that I took from the office." She nodded toward Mr. Kingsley and continued.

"Tonight I found a wadded-up piece of paper in the garbage at the office. I think Claudette wrote the note." Lucy uncrumpled the note. "And I think she left the bottle with the note in it on my porch when you two visited on Tuesday," she said to Claudette's mom.

Mr. Kingsley looked upset—really upset. "I did give Claudette some of the bottles after you left on Saturday," Mr. Kingsley said. "I'm so sorry. She felt left out, and I wanted her to have some. I'll speak with her about this right now."

"Please wait!" Lucy held up her hand. "I think you're right. She felt left out, and that part was my fault. I'm not mad at her. In fact, I totally understand. I'd like to talk to her myself, if that's okay."

Mrs. Kingsley looked at her husband, who agreed. "We'll still have to talk about it with her later," she said.

Lucy nodded. "And would it be okay if she came to my party? I'm sure my mom and dad will say that we can bring her home."

Mrs. Kingsley nodded. "It's kind of you to think of

Claudette on your birthday. Especially with this note."

Lucy smiled. She thought about the summers before, and pedal boating, and Claudette's crazy sock combinations. "Until tonight, I didn't realize how much like a little sister Claudette really is to me."

Lucy opened the living room door and walked upstairs. She knocked on Claudette's door.

Claudette opened the door. "Lucy!" she squealed. "Why aren't you at your party?"

Lucy entered the room, with its neon pink, yellow, and orange decorations stuck all around. Claudette had a rack of different-colored jump ropes hooked on her wall; the ropes all tilted downward like a rainbow of frowns, one on top of the other.

Lucy sat down on Claudette's bed and patted the space beside her. Claudette came over and sat down.

"Do you know what this is?" Lucy unfolded the crumpled ball. Inside the folds you could easily read *Stop the Parte.*

"Oh," Claudette frowned. Her chin quivered. "I guess you're not here to see my new jump rope song."

Lucy shook her head.

Claudette started to cry. "I'm really sorry, Lucy. As soon as my mom and I walked away from your house, I wanted to run back and get that thing and throw it away. But then I'd have to tell my mom why I wanted to go back." She kept talking through her sobs. "And I knew I would get in big trouble. I was hoping that it would sink to the bottom of the bush and no one would find it till after you moved home at the end of the summer."

"I'm not mad at you anymore."

Claudette grabbed a tissue and noisily blew her nose. "You're not?"

Lucy shook her head again.

"I know how you feel. I don't have a brother or a sister, either, so we can both get pretty lonely, can't we?"

Claudette nodded and started sniffling again. "But you have Serena, so I don't have anyone, not even you!"

Lucy smiled. "What about Betsy's little sister? What was her name?"

"Michelle. But I don't know her last name, and I don't know where she lives. My mom can't call her or anything to see if she can play."

"Well, I'm really sorry, too, Claudette," Lucy said. "I was so busy worrying about *me* feeling lonely and never belonging that I didn't stop to think you probably feel the same way."

"I do," Claudette cried. "And we always used to spend our birthdays together. Even if we never get parties 'cause we're always away." She stood up and threw away her tissue, pulling a new one out of a silver foil tissue box. Then she sat down next to Lucy again.

"We need our own friends, because I'm older than you are. We can't spend every minute together, and I'll still be with Serena a lot. But I'll help fix things up with Michelle, and you and I can be special friends. Like a big sister and a little sister, okay?"

Claudette smiled again. "Okay."

"And," Lucy continued, "we always *do* spend our birthdays together. Not *used to*. And this year we'll both have a party."

"Really?" Claudette said.

"Really. And you're coming to my party tonight. I already asked your mom and dad." Lucy smiled at the unmixed joy that shone on Claudette's face. "But first, I have a present for you."

Claudette's joy was catching. Lucy felt it spread across her face and reach down to her heart. She reached into her pocket and pulled out the second Wired for Christ necklace. She leaned over and handed it to Claudette.

"Remember when you bought me the glow-in-the-dark cross last week so we could be matchies?" she asked.

Claudette nodded.

"Well, here's a necklace for you that matches mine." Lucy reached under her shirt and pulled her own necklace out to show Claudette.

Claudette clasped the necklace between her hands and closed her eyes in delight. "Will you put it on me?"

Lucy snapped the necklace around Claudette's neck. "Now, you need to get changed if you want to go to the party."

"Will there be lots of kids there?" Claudette asked.

Lucy drew a deep breath and let it slowly escape. "I don't know," she answered. "Maybe ten girls, maybe no one besides you and me and Serena. There's a lot of food if nobody shows up."

"Well, we can all eat a *lot* if no one else comes. Then everything will be okay," Claudette said.

Lucy smiled and tousled Claudette's hair. *I guess I won't have time to do the other thing I need to do* before *the party. Maybe it will happen* at *the party*, she thought, worry tightening her chest.

The Party

Friday evening . . .

A few minutes later, Claudette and Lucy walked into the front room of their dads' office, where the party was to be held. Everyone was on the patio, so the two girls walked out to the back.

"Lucy!" her mother said. "I was worried about you. You can't just go off without telling anyone where you're going!"

"I'm sorry, Mom," she said. "I thought I'd be here before you guys got back. I wanted to go and get Claudette for the party."

Serena raised her eyebrows.

Lucy mouthed, "I'll tell you later."

"Look how beautiful everything is!" Claudette said. She wandered around the patio admiring everything. Lucy smiled at Claudette's outfit. Baby blue shorts, baby blue shirt. Black-and-pink-striped socks.

Claudette popped a piece of watermelon in her mouth. "It's okay to eat something, isn't it?" she asked.

"Yes," Lucy's dad said. The grill sat to the side of the patio. He wore an apron and made sure the smoke was being funneled away from the patio. And Lucy knew there were a lot of burgers sitting on a tray in the fridge, waiting to be cooked.

Lucy checked the time. *Someone should be here by now.*

"Don't worry," Serena whispered. "It will be a good time, no matter what." The music seemed loud, with so few voices.

Then the doorbell rang.

Lucy and Serena ran to the front. At least *someone* was coming.

It was Betsy. And her little sister, Michelle.

"Come in!" Lucy said. She pulled Betsy into the front room.

"Michelle!" Claudette said, running toward the door. Michelle ran to meet her and gave her a big hug.

"I hope it's okay that I brought her. I wasn't sure," Betsy said, her long braids coiled in the back today with little flower clips stuck here and there. "My life is never my own. I exist to baby-sit."

"It's perfect," Lucy reassured her. "My 'little sister' is here, too. It will keep them busy."

Betsy handed a small box to Lucy. "Here's a little present. I know you said you didn't want anything, but these were small, and I wanted to get them."

"Thank you," Lucy said, her voice softer. "Come on in."

Lucy, Serena, and Betsy walked out to the patio and sat down, chatting about their summer plans, friends at home, and hair troubles. A few minutes later the doorbell rang again.

Lucy's heart skipped a beat.

She and Serena opened the door. "Lydia, Kelly!" Serena said, filling in the names.

Lucy was so glad, because she recognized their faces from the beach last week but didn't remember their names.

"Our moms called your mom," they said to Serena. "And she told them she knew Lucy's mother. So we were allowed to come! We brought the Make a Mystery game to play. I hope that's okay," Kelly said, holding out a box.

"It's a great idea." Lucy stepped forward. She was *so* thankful that Serena's mom had come on the boat! "I'm Lucy, in case you don't remember, since we only met once. Thanks for coming."

"Sure." Lydia and Kelly smiled. They didn't look upset. Not like someone had threatened them if they didn't come.

"Let's go out back," Lucy said.

Thank you, God. Even if only three girls come, that means there are five of us plus Michelle and Claudette. You are so good.

After half an hour, Lucy's dad said, "Well, I guess I'll put the burgers on." He looked at Lucy, but she wasn't upset. They were having a great time playing Make a Mystery together.

"Okay, Dad," she said. Serena changed the CD to something quieter while they played. Claudette and Michelle giggled from the other room.

And then, when they were just about to eat, the doorbell rang again.

When Lucy and Serena answered it, there was a crowd. In front of the crowd was the smallest of all, Jenny.

"I'm sorry we're late," she said. "I waited at my house for everyone to come together, in case people hadn't heard that we're going to your party tonight instead."

"*Our* party," Lucy said, reaching for her hand. Behind Jenny were Amy, Erica, and another girl whose name Lucy couldn't remember. Erica didn't look too happy, and she was sticking with Amy. But at least she came.

"This is my mom and dad," Jenny said.

"Thanks for having us come," her mom spoke up. "We felt so bad when Jenny's grandpa got sick. But then your mom came by this afternoon to make sure we would come. I wasn't sure it was okay, but she seemed so warm and welcoming. We thought, well, why not?"

"No trouble! It's more fun with everyone," Lucy said, her heart like an overblown balloon, stretched with delight, light with joy. *Mom helped with the party! Yahoo!* Lucy took Jenny's parents into the back to the kitchen.

"Shoo! Get out of the kitchen!" her mother said as Lucy tried to enter. Then her mother saw Jenny's mom. "Oh, I'm so sorry, come on in." She looked at the girls. "If you're over thirty years old, that is. Good to see you again."

"How did you know to ask her?" Lucy whispered to her mother before leaving the room.

"The note on the refrigerator door had her name and address—and you told me it was Jenny, remember?" Mom whispered back. "I sped over there this afternoon while you guys were decorating. I know I haven't done much for the party. But all of a sudden I thought, 'I could help with this.' "

Lucy kissed her mother's cheek. Then she and the other girls giggled and ran back to the patio, scooting to make room for the new girls as they finished the Make a Mystery game.

Everyone we invited is here. Except Julie, Lucy thought. Would Julie show up at all, make a big scene in the midst of everything? Or stay away altogether?

Soon the burgers were done. Jenny's parents had stayed, as they'd told the parents of the girls they had invited to their party they would.

"It kind of worked out nice," Lucy whispered to Serena as she put ketchup on her burger. "I mean, all the parents let the kids come, because they knew Jenny's mom and dad already, even if they didn't know me."

"It all did work out right, didn't it?" Serena whispered back.

The girls took their paper plates out to the soft green grass and picnicked together. They chatted about the summer camp on the Island that some of them were going to go to in a few weeks.

"We're going to have water-skiing and skeet shooting and lots of other stuff," Lydia said. "At least we did last year."

"Don't forget about Horse Heaven," Kelly said, watermelon juice coursing down her chin.

"What's Horse Heaven?" Lucy asked.

"My mom runs it," Kelly said after wiping her chin with a napkin. "It's in the interior, where most of the horses are boarded. You learn about horses for a week and care for your own. There are even overnight riding trails."

"Cool! Can I come?"

Kelly promised to ask her mother about it. Lydia said she'd check into the camp and talk with the rest of them about it sometime when they saw each other on the beach.

"Lucy!" her mother called out. "Someone is at the door."

Lucy set her plate down. Everyone she'd invited was already there. Except for one.

"I'll come, too," Serena said. More than anything, Lucy felt like running in the other direction.

They picked their way through the other girls, stepping in between. When Lucy got to the door, she froze.

"Hi, Dr Pepper!" Jake said.

"Hi, Jake," Lucy said. "What are you doing here?" She realized how rude that sounded. "I mean, how did you know we were here?" That sounded dumb, too. *Mama mia!*

"You told me your birthday party was Friday night, remember?"

"Oh yeah," Lucy said. "Would you like to come in?" she asked.

"No thanks. I'm on my way to a friend's house. It's just that my dad's order of Jelly Bellies came in today, and I remembered that you'd wanted some." He held out a little plastic teddy bear filled with Jelly Bellies.

"They're Dr Pepper flavored. I might not have thought about bringing these to you, except when I was unpacking and saw this flavor, it reminded me."

Lucy reached out and took the bear. Serena stood a little to the side.

"Well, thanks," Lucy said.

"No problem," Jake said, heading back down the sidewalk. "Have a happy birthday!"

"Wow!" Serena said. "Smooth."

"It's not a big deal, okay?" Lucy said under her breath. Secretly, she thought it was nice that anyone cared enough to remember what she liked and bring something for her birthday.

"He's a nice friend," Serena agreed.

When they got back to the patio, Serena changed the CD to one with a beat while the other girls threw away their dinner garbage.

"We haven't danced yet!" Lucy said. "The girls in the diary did the one-step!"

Claudette overheard and asked, "What's a one-step?" Then she hopped all over the patio floor on one foot. "Like this?"

Erica laughed. "I don't know how to do the one-step, but I know how to do the Cabbage Patch."

All nine big girls and the two little ones watched as Erica taught them the Cabbage Patch. Then Amy taught them the Chicken.

"Come on, Jenny. It's your birthday, too. You go first," Amy said. Jenny blushed and went out to the middle. When she started dancing everyone clapped. She was great!

"I didn't know you could dance so well," Lydia said. Jenny blushed some more.

"Okay, how about the Sprinkler," Lucy said. She got

out to the middle and put her hand to the side of her head and moved her elbow like a sprinkler going around and around watering the yard.

Everyone laughed and sprinkled, too, loosened up by the festive mood and music.

"What a party!" Serena sighed. "It wasn't the one-step, but you do know how to dance!"

The girls sat down and fanned themselves. In a minute, Lucy's mother came out with the cake. She motioned for the girls to circle around a table.

"Lucy and Jenny, come up front," Lucy's dad called.

As Lucy got closer, she could see something was written on that cake!

"Hey," she said.

"I ran to the store this afternoon and got some icing pens," her mother whispered. In bright red icing on the cake her mother had written *Happy 12th Birthdays, Jenny and Lucy.*

Jenny glowed like the twenty-four candles on the cake.

"Don't forget to make a wish," Serena called out after they sang "The Birthday Song" but before the girls blew out the candles.

Jenny closed her eyes. *Making a wish, I'll bet*, Lucy thought.

Then Lucy closed her eyes and made her own wish.

This is the best birthday ever. I hope this will be the best summer ever. It's my birthday wish.

"Don't tell your wish!" Serena said.

"I won't," Jenny said, and Lucy nodded.

I won't tell, but I'll hold that wish close to my heart every week.

After a bit, Jenny's parents said they had to get back to check on her grandpa, and that they'd walk the girls home.

Lucy came forward and stood at the door, handing each girl a puka shell anklet as they left.

"There's one for everyone to wear, so no one feels left out," she said as they filed through the door to go home. She slipped the extra one into her pocket.

"Thanks, Lucy!" Most of the girls stopped right outside the door and fastened their anklets on.

"Roberto is coming to take me home and pick up our stereo," Serena said. "But first we have to read the rest of our diary, right? To see if the old diary's party was as fun as ours."

"Right!" Lucy said, eyes shining.

"I'm going to take Claudette home," Lucy's dad said. "I'll be back."

"I'll clean up and then we'll go home, too," her mom said, giving Lucy a big, squeezy hug.

"I'm going to the beach with Serena for a minute, Mom. But before I can go home tonight, I have to make one important stop first. It's really close, just a couple blocks away," Lucy said. "I have to take care of it tonight."

"What is it?" her mom said.

"I need to face the one girl who didn't show up tonight," Lucy said.

Wishes

Friday night . . .

Lucy and Serena walked barefoot down to the beach behind the office, toting the old diary, which Lucy had brought from home.

The cool sand rolled beneath their soles and between their toes, squashing down as they walked. They found a place where the moonlight wasn't blocked by palm trees, so they could see to read. Then they sat down together.

"It was great, wasn't it?" Serena asked.

Lucy grinned. "It was great."

Serena dug her toes into the sand and wrote her name with her pointer finger. "Remember last time we drew letters in the sand and you worried about belonging?"

"Yes," Lucy said. She had written the word *B-E-L-O-N-G.* "I'm so glad a lot of people came. But even if they hadn't, I'd feel good. Having this party helped me figure out that I already belong a lot of places. With my mom and dad, no matter what's up with them. My mom did the invitations, even though she doesn't like parties. My dad let us use this place, and so much more."

Serena nodded.

Lucy continued. "I see I belong with Claudette, and she with me. I see I belong with Jesus. And we can get even closer." Lucy touched her new necklace.

She turned toward Serena. "And I belong with you. I guess when I started to understand that, I didn't feel as desperate anymore."

Serena smiled, and Lucy cracked open the old red leather diary and found the page where they'd left off.

" 'Well, the party *was* a panic,' " Mary's handwriting said as Lucy read aloud.

> "Everyone came, and we ate and danced because the radio worked! It started out shaky, but we made a tall tower and set it on top. Once we did that, New York City came through like a dream. The food was the bee's knees and Serena's dancing — what a hoofer!"

A few paragraphs talked about who was there, what they did, who showed up, and who would have the next party. Lucy came to the end of the paragraph and read, " 'This promises to be a great summer, except . . .' "

Serena looked at Lucy. "Except what?"

Lucy handed over the diary. "Your turn to read. The handwriting changes."

"Except that next week we begin the new project.

It is very important, but also could be trouble, because no one wants to think about it. Mary and I are determined to help, no matter what trouble it causes."

The handwriting changed back. Lucy read:

"I hope it doesn't cause much trouble. I don't like trouble. We'll write soon, diary. With love and affection, the faithful friends. Mary and Serena.

Lucy closed the diary, as there was nothing else on that page. The next page held the next week's adventure. "Trouble!" she said triumphantly. "Trouble sounds like an adventure."

Serena put her head in her hands. "I'm with Mary," she said. "I don't like trouble."

Lucy giggled. "It will be fun. Like the Make a Mystery game. Except real!"

Serena looked up and smiled. "Don't go planning *more* trouble than we need."

"We'll find out tomorrow when we open the diary for next week's Diary Deed," Lucy said. She cracked open their own diary. "I haven't written in this yet."

She took a pencil she'd brought for that purpose and wrote beneath the doodle Serena had drawn on the boat.

Diary, this night turned out fantabulous! Everything went great, in spite of my major worries. We didn't do the

*one-step (ha-ha), but we did the Sprinkler. Lots of people
came, and I even got a present from Serena's friend Jake.
I guess he's my friend, too. Anyway, Julie didn't come.
I'll . . . um, write more about that later. Next week—
trouble ahead!*

Lucy wrote down a few more things, and then Serena
jotted down a few words before signing off, too.

"Hey, I haven't given you your birthday present yet,"
Serena said as she closed their diary and set it aside. She
held out a thin envelope she must have snuck down to the
beach.

"Thanks!" Lucy slit open the side of the envelope and
drew out a piece of paper. On it was a pencil sketch of her
and Serena, sitting on the beach.

"This is soooo great!" Lucy said. "How did you draw
this?"

"From the picture Philip took of us. First I just planned
to frame it and give it to you as a present. Then I saw my
sketchbook and thought how encouraging you were to me.
So I drew it for you. I hope it's not a stupid birthday present."

Lucy hugged her friend. "It's a wonderful birthday present."

The water rolled in. "Speaking of stupidity," Lucy said.
"Mine, that is. I'd better get going to Julie's house. I have
to apologize for blaming her."

"Blaming her for what?" Serena asked.

"Well, I haven't mentioned it yet, but I got a note sent
in a bottle telling me to stop the party."

"NO!"

"Well, I did. I, um, thought it was best to handle it myself."

Serena shook her head.

"Anyway," Lucy continued, "I thought it was Julie. I . . . uh, I called her and told her I knew she'd sent that mean note." Lucy hung her head.

"Uh-oh. It wasn't her, then?"

"No, it was Claudette."

Serena's mouth opened, and then she closed it and nodded. "So that's why you ran off to get her tonight."

Lucy smiled. "Yes, but now I need to go apologize to Julie."

"Do you want me to come?" Serena asked.

"No thanks."

"You don't have to do everything on your own, you know."

Lucy said nothing for a minute, but she didn't say she agreed, either. "Well, *this* time I'm taking my dad. Just in case . . ."

Serena smiled. "I'll be gone when you get back. Roberto will be here in a minute. But we'll meet tomorrow and read the next section of the diary."

"The *trouble* section," Lucy reminded her, teasing.

Serena rolled her eyes.

"One last thing," Lucy said, moving closer to the water and the wet sand. "I want to see if those electric bugs really work."

She drew F-A-I-T-H-F-U-L in the wet sand, watching

the letters light up. The little phosphorescent bugs trailed her finger. "Cool!"

Serena came alongside her and wrote *F-R-I-E-N-D-S*. It lit up, too.

The two of them laughed. "It's me and you, Faithful Friends," Lucy said as they walked back to the office.

When they got there, the patio was dark and Lucy's parents stood in the front room. Lucy's dad had already taken Claudette home.

"I'm packed up. Everything is in the basket in the back of the golf cart," Lucy's mother said. "Shall we drop you off on our way?" she asked Serena.

"My brother, Roberto, is coming. I'm sorry he isn't here yet," Serena said, kind of panicked. "He's always late."

"We can wait."

Lucy looked at the clock. Soon it would be too late to get to Julie's.

"Would it be okay if Dad came with me for a minute to talk to that one girl?" she asked.

"If they go, Roberto and I can drop you off at home," Serena said to Lucy's mother. "He's bringing our golf cart."

Lucy's mother nodded. Serena reminded Lucy where Julie lived.

"See you tomorrow," Serena said.

Lucy smiled and squeezed her friend's hand. Then she and her dad stepped into the cart and headed toward Julie's house.

A few minutes later, he turned the golf cart off.

"I'll be right back," Lucy said. She stepped through the night up to Julie's townhouse. A blue TV glow came from the front window. She knocked.

Julie answered. "Oh. You."

Lucy said. "I came to tell you that I'm sorry I accused you of sending me a mean note. I was wrong. Will you forgive me?"

Julie's face froze. Maybe no one had ever apologized to her.

"Yeah," she said. Behind her, Lucy could see Julie's mother yakking on the phone, a haze of tobacco smoke around her head.

"Anyway, I'm sorry you couldn't come tonight, but I brought something for you." Lucy reached into her pocket and drew out the last anklet. "I bought one for everyone. I didn't want you to feel left out if you saw people wearing them."

Julie didn't say anything. But she opened her palm and let Lucy drop it in. She curled her hand around it, but not too tightly.

"See you later," Lucy said.

Julie's face still looked cold, but she waved.

Lucy sat down in the golf cart, and her dad started it up. "Everything go okay?" her dad said.

Lucy nodded.

"Hey, where's the flower?" He pointed at her ear, where he'd placed the flower earlier that day.

"I . . . ah, gave it away," Lucy said.

At the next stop sign, Dad hopped out and snapped another stem from the vase in the basket in the back of the cart, where the party gear was packed up. Then he hopped into the cart and stuck it behind her ear again.

"Better?" he said.

"Better." Lucy grinned. As they cruised down the road past the beach, she looked at the gently rolling water, the silent boats, and felt the warm night. Lydia was checking on camp, and Kelly on horses.

Serena and Lucy had trouble ahead next week. Lucy felt goose bumps rise.

Her wish, for the best summer ever, might just come true after all.

Draw close to God,
and God will draw close to you.

JAMES 4:8

The best birthday parties SANDRA BYRD ever had were sleepovers with three girls plus herself. What are the best things they did? They made up crazy dances, tried new hairdos, and told mystery stories late into the night. No one ever showed up with Jelly Bellies, though.

Sandra lives near beautiful Seattle, between the snow-capped Mount Rainier and the Space Needle, with her husband and two children (and let's not forget her Australian Shepherd, Trudy). When she's not writing, she's usually reading, but she also likes to scrapbook, listen to music, and spend time with friends. Besides writing THE HIDDEN DIARY books, she's also the author of the bestselling series SECRET SISTERS.

For more information on THE HIDDEN DIARY series, visit Sandra's Web site: *www.thehiddendiary.com.*

**Don't miss book three
of THE HIDDEN DIARY,
Just Between Friends!**

For a preview of Lucy and Serena's next diary adventure, just hold up this page in front of a mirror.

What could be more heartbreaking than a little lost dog? A hurt, little lost dog? Things can get messy, and Lucy bargains for trouble. . . .